Wasted

Wasted

Brent R. Sherrard

James Lorimer & Company Ltd., Publishers
Toronto

James Lorimer & Company Ltd. acknowledges the support of the
Canada Council for the Arts and the Ontario Arts Council for our
publishing program. We acknowlcdge the financial support of the
Government of Canada through the Book Publishing Industry
Development Program (BPIDP) for our publishing activities.We
acknowledge the Government of Ontario through the Ontario
Media Development Corporation's Ontario Book Initiative.\

Library and Archives Canada Cataloguing in Publication
Wasted / Brent R. Sherrard.
(SideStreets)

ISBN 978-1-55277-420-5 (bound).—ISBN 978-1-55277-419-9 (pbk.)

I. Title. II. Series: SideStreets

PS8637.H488W37 2009 jC813'.6 C2009-901668-0

James Lorimer & Company Ltd.,
Publishers
317 Adelaide Street West
Suite 1002
Toronto, Ontario
M5V 1P9
www.lorimer.ca

Distributed in the
U.S. by:
Orca Book Publishers
P.O. Box 468
Custer, WA USA
98240-0468

Printed and bound in Canada.

*In fond memory of Warren C. Jardine,
friend and hero.*

Much love and thanks to my wife, friend and soul-mate, Valerie. Life is good.

A big thank you to my editor Faye Smailes, who helped make the book a reality.

And thanks to my Posse. Most inspiring.

Chapter 1

It's amazing how something that someone else does can affect your life so much. Take my Uncle Ralph, for example. He had his own accounting business, and thought that he'd discovered a fool-proof way of stealing his clients' income-tax payments, outsmarting both his clients and the government. He'd been doing it for a while before a random audit on a customer of his revealed that the government had no record of the income tax they'd paid for the last three years, much to their surprise. Uncle Ralph was investigated and busted for numerous counts of fraud.

That was a bad thing for Ralph, but a good thing for me, because if he hadn't got busted, I wouldn't be telling this story. I'd be dead.

It was my seventeenth birthday, and I was celebrating by helping my old man change the transmission in his pickup. I was lying on my back under the truck, trying to hold the thing up in the air while Dad swore at me for being so weak as he tried to get the bolts that attached it to the engine started into the holes. I was thinking that if he would slam back a few more beers to quell the shaking in his hands he'd maybe quit dropping the darned things, and I could enjoy the hot and humid Saturday by getting drunk myself. After all, it *was* my birthday.

He finally got two of the bolts started, which was enough to keep the transmission from falling on my chest and crushing me if I let go. I crawled out from under the truck, covered in sweat and grease and transmission fluid, to find Dad handing me a beer. I was hungover from the night before, so I really appreciated it. I figured he must finally consider me a man, and took a seat beside him on the tailgate. Maybe now he would start calling me Jacob, instead of "Idiot," or "Peckerhead."

We sat there drinking in silence since we had never really had what you'd call a close relationship. If he hadn't needed a hand fixing the truck, we would have been ignoring each other, like we always did. I heard the crunch of tires on gravel, and had a momentary hope that it might be one of my friends coming to rescue me. Looking up, I saw a late model Lexus with Ontario licence plates pulling into our driveway. *Another tourist, lost and looking for directions*, I figured.

The windows of the car were smoked glass, and with the sun hitting the windshield from an angle it was impossible to see inside. The driver's side door opened and a woman stepped out from behind the wheel, tossing big drugstore-blond curls and tipping back designer sunglasses with practised coolness. Dad swore, and I realized that it was my Aunt Corrine. No one had mentioned that she was coming down from Toronto, and I breathed a sigh of relief that my cousin Rufus wasn't with her. But my relief was short-lived. The passenger door opened and Rufus stepped out into the oppressive heat, looking like he smelled something bad, just like I remembered him.

"I don't see that idiot, anyway," Dad said, referring to my pompous Uncle Ralph — who, unknown to us, was sitting in a Toronto holding cell at that very moment. Dad drained his beer and tossed the bottle over his shoulder in the general direction of the woods behind us, then released a massive belch. He didn't care much for anyone in my mom's family, including Mom, but Aunt Corrine was his least favourite.

"Angie's in the house. I gotta take a leak," he announced, staggering slightly as he ambled over to the back of the woodshed. He would come back reeking of cheap whisky, and flaunting an attitude that showed the world just what he thought of everyone and everything.

"How are you, Jacob?" inquired Corrine as she shook her head in disgust and started toward the house. Rufus didn't even toss a look in my direction as he followed her. Maybe it was the beer in my hand, which I knew they'd both find shocking, or maybe they were judging me by the company I kept. Regardless of their reasons, I wasn't about to let them affect me.

"I'm fine, Corrine, thank you. It's nice to see you again, a really nice surprise. How are you doing, Rufus?"

"Good," he replied, still failing to make eye contact.

"You're not going in the house with the ladies, are you?" I asked. I knew I had him; he'd pretty well have to admit he was one of the girls if he went in.

"I need to use the washroom," he replied, casting me a sullen look over his shoulder. Apparently city boys couldn't piss in the woods.

I drained my beer, which was quickly growing warm. August in New Brunswick can be brutally hot, with hazy skies and little breeze, and so much moisture in the air that you feel like you are trapped under a warm, wet blanket. I headed for the back of the shed to take a leak and found Dad on his hands and knees, heaving like a broken-winded horse. It was too hot for a lot of activities, and it was plain to see that guzzling straight whisky was one of them. I waited until he'd caught his breath, then helped him into the shade. I retrieved the whisky bottle and re-capped it, then placed it next to him against the wall of the shed. It was going to be a long day.

I turned my attention back to the truck. Since

the transmission had been secured, there was the matter of putting the rest of the housing bolts in place, and re-attaching the driveshaft and shifting mechanism. If I didn't do it, we'd have no vehicle for days, seeing as Dad wouldn't be capable of doing much until he got himself straightened out a bit. He had driven home from his buddy's house two days before — twenty minutes of his foot flat on the mat with the truck in low gear. You could hear the metal grinding as he pulled into the yard, oblivious to everything but the bottle between his knees. It was amazing that he hadn't killed himself, or someone else, but I knew that one of these times his luck would run out, and we'd be left in peace.

I slid back under the truck and was just getting the first bolt tightened when I heard, "Is there anything I can do to help?" It was Rufus.

It came as a bit of a shock that he'd offer to do anything that might get his hands dirty, or anything that might be considered work. I was surprised that he'd even found the guts to come back outside. "No, not right now. But in a few minutes I could use an extra hand getting the driveshaft back in place," I said.

I finished up with the transmission, making small talk about the weather, which Rufus responded to with small answers. It was easier for us to be able to get the preliminaries out of the way without having to make eye contact — more for him than me. As I emerged from under the truck I got my first real look at him, and was puzzled by the expression on his face. I couldn't tell if he was worried, or just plain pissed-off. Either way, it was an improvement over his usual spoiled, snotty look.

"I'm going to have one of Dad's beers," I said. "You want one? He'll never notice them gone. What do you say?"

He surprised me again by saying yes. So we sat in the shed, clear of his mother's view, and popped two bottles open. His Toronto and my Miramichi, New Brunswick, were two separate worlds actually, and the distance left us both feeling pretty awkward. I decided that the most obvious question would be why he was here. So I asked, and his answer, just three simple words, would become the reason why I'm still here to tell this story.

"Dad got arrested," he replied.

Chapter 2

"Arrested? No kidding. For *what*?" I couldn't imagine what his father, an accountant who spent most of his spare time in slippers in front of a TV or computer screen, could've possibly been nailed for.

"Breach of trust, misappropriation of funds. You know, theft of his clients' money, to put it in real terms. It's really bad, the federal government's even involved. It's a mess, Jacob. He's facing prison time."

He let out a huge sigh. I really did feel bad for him, although I was hoping that he wasn't going to start crying or anything. Dad had got sixty days in jail the year before on a DUI, his third, and I'd been glad to see him go. But Ralph wasn't a drunk who drove his family crazy, so I knew that I wasn't looking at it from the same angle as Rufus was.

"Well, innocent until proven guilty, right?"

I said.

"Yeah, I guess," Rufus replied, although he sounded like he had no doubt that Ralph really was guilty. I realized that I'd always considered him much younger than me, even though he was actually twelve days older. It was because he'd always lived an easy life, one that left him soft. A *safe* life. Compared to my friends and me, he *was* young — you could see it in his eyes. But his faith in that life had been shaken, and now he was facing blunt reality. *Welcome to the real world, Rufus*, I thought.

We sipped our beer and kicked the dirt floor, while I thought back to the last time he'd been to New Brunswick.

It had been four years earlier, the summer that we'd both turned thirteen. My friends and I had already started hanging out, getting wasted on booze that we'd stolen from our fathers, and smoking anything that we could lay our hands on. In our way of thinking we were becoming men, following the only example we'd ever known.

I had convinced Aunt Corrine to allow Rufus to go along with me to my best friend Bobby Glenwood's place, telling her that we'd be playing ball, or some other lie, and that I would have him home by ten o'clock. In reality, we were heading for the woods behind Bobby's house, where my buddies and I had built a fire pit from slabs of shale rock that we'd lugged from the

16

riverbank. It was a Saturday night, and we'd all spent the week squirrelling away a variety of booze.

We had only been there a short while, with Rufus looking like he was about to puke from nerves, when Larry Simms showed up. He was already half wasted and, as usual, looking for a fight. He'd grown up with an abusive father, which was no big deal around Miramichi, and three older brothers who used him as a punching bag. So, basically, he was always looking to make someone else pay for his suffering. He was tough, and won most of his fights on sheer guts.

"Whose woman is this?" he said as soon as he spotted Rufus. Of course everyone laughed, and Rufus looked like he was going to pass out.

"Leave him be," I said, hoping that maybe Larry would back off, but knowing better.

"Well, I guess that answers my question, don't it?" he replied, to another round of laughter.

"He's my cousin, just down from Toronto for a visit, Larry. They're going back in a few days. Give him a break, would you?" I had hoped I might get Rufus out of there quickly, before Larry really got started, but it had been too late.

"Oh, Toronto, eh?" Larry had turned on Rufus in a flash. "I bet you think we're a bunch of backwoods hicks, don't you? I bet you think you're better than we are, right? Well, you're not, and I'll prove that right here now. I'll give

17

you a souvenir to take back to the city with you, something to show the rest of your sissy friends. How about that?"

Larry reached into his pocket and swaggered over to Rufus, who stood staring at the ground with his mouth hanging open. When the hand came out of his pocket, it was clenched into a tight fist, which Larry held up like the souvenir was inside. Then it smashed into Rufus's face, knocking him flat in the dirt. Blood started gushing out of his lip where a tooth had gone through, and he was squealing like a wounded pig.

Before I realized what I was doing, I rushed over and shoved Larry, who had been reaching down to pull Rufus back onto his feet for more punishment. It had been bad enough to hit someone who was basically defenceless, but just plain stupid to continue the abuse.

I fought back, but it was no use. In no time I had a bloody nose, my ears were ringing, and both of my eyes were swelling up, but at least I'd showed courage by trying. Larry finally stopped punching and offered me his hand, and as I reached out to shake it, he smiled and slammed me one more shot in the face. Typical Larry.

I helped Rufus up from where he was lying, rolled into a protective ball, the whole time that I'd been accepting his pounding, and we headed for home. He cried all the way. When we got back to the house he really turned on the tears, *sobbing and shaking while his mother tried to soothe him. "You people," she kept saying over and over again, as if she hadn't spent the first twenty years of her life in the same area, like we were savages that she simply couldn't understand. Uncle Ralph wanted to call the police, and Dad just shook his head in disgust. The family packed up and left in the morning, swearing that they'd never come back to this "God-forsaken hell hole." I watched them leave through eyes that were nearly swelled shut, and figured I'd never see them again. At least Rufus could've said thank you.*

Now, I glanced over at Rufus, sitting on the toolbox looking so pitiful, and imagined that he did think we were a bunch of backwoods hicks. And he wouldn't be wrong. Here I was on my birthday, with no plans for the future but getting wasted. Dad was passed out drunk behind the shed, and our family vehicle was a rusted-out, oil-guzzling pickup truck. Suddenly, I felt like I was the one who should be ashamed.

"So, how long are you guys here for?" I asked, trying to break the awkward tension.

"Just for a few days, maybe a week," he replied. "Mom said that she had to get away, I think more from embarrassment than anything. I wish that I could get away forever. I can't take it much longer, Jacob. I can't make a move without him jumping on me. I hope they lock him up for good, the arrogant bastard."

"Well, you can always come stay with us," I joked.

"Thanks, Jacob. I just might take you up on that offer."

A shadow fell over us, and I looked up to see Dad, whisky bottle in his hand and grass stains on his face.

"Gotta shange that transhmishim, boy," he said, and fell into the wall. "No damn good."

I figured that last statement was meant for me. He was totally pissed, again, and it was time to clear out of there before we were subjected to his alcoholic wisdom. I didn't even bother trying to tell him that the transmission job was already done. I'd have to wait until he sobered up enough to understand, whenever that might be.

"Let's get that driveshaft in place, before it gets any hotter," I said to Rufus, ignoring Dad, who was using the shed wall to keep himself from top-pling over. "Then we can go celebrate my birthday."

Within fifteen sweat-drenched minutes I had the truck mobile again. Dad was nowhere in sight as I crawled out from under the truck, and Rufus went into the shed to clean his hands while I took the keys in to my mother. The last thing we needed was for the old man to go for another booze cruise. I was reaching for the doorknob when I heard a crash.

"Oh God, oh my God!" I heard Rufus yell. I bounded to the shed door, where we both stared in horror at the sight of Dad, flat on his back in the dirt, the handle of a screwdriver sticking out of his chest.

Chapter 3

"Quick, grab his feet. We'll put him on the back of the truck," I ordered Rufus, who surprised me by being able to respond at all. "We've got to get him to the hospital, fast."

We managed to get him loaded into the truck, and I told Rufus to hold his head as I jumped into the cab and tore out of the driveway. It was a fifteen-minute drive to the hospital, and I knew that the black-handled screwdriver must've nearly gone clean through him, as the shaft was almost a foot long. As panicked as I was, I couldn't help but think that he'd probably been trying to pop open a beer with it, even though they all had twist-off tops. I'd seen the unopened bottle lying on the floor next to him.

I slid the truck to a stop at the hospital doors leading into Emergency, jumped out, and crashed through them into the lobby. "My dad fell on a screwdriver, it's in his chest, he's on the truck, quick!" I yelled at the nurse on duty behind the desk, who immediately sprang into action.

Operating like a well-trained pit crew, within minutes they had him strapped to a rolling stretcher and whisked away behind closed doors. I headed for the payphone to call Mom and give her the bad news, but Rufus offered me his cell phone instead. I felt like an idiot when I had to get him to explain how to use it.

"Fell on a screwdriver? What was he doing? How bad is it? You've got the *truck*?" she asked, unaware that we'd even left.

"It's really bad, Mom. He's headed for surgery, so there's no hurry for you to get here. Rufus and I will hang around. I can keep you informed, you know, if you'd rather not come down." As I said it, I felt like maybe it was a stupid thing to say. Of course she'd want to be here, close by, where a wife belonged.

"No," she said, sounding more disgusted than concerned. "I *have* to come down. I'll be there in a while. Corrine can bring me and Jenny. "

Jenny was my little sister, twelve years old and already jaded by the life that had been forced upon her. She spent most of her time with her nose buried in a book, and I worried about how long it would be before she found a more exciting — and dangerous — method of escape.

I went outside for a smoke, and found Rufus sitting on the curb, holding his head in his hands. I moved the truck over into the parking area and took a seat on the tailgate, in the shade of a huge maple tree. There wasn't a hint of a breeze, and the sweat clung to my skin like puke to a blanket.

"Is he going to be all right?" Rufus asked as he came over. "He's not going to die, is he?"

"With any luck," I said, leaving him to ponder which question I'd answered.

I sat there dragging on the cigarette, reflecting on the life that we led, all of it directly related to Dad's addiction. I tried, but failed, to dredge up any happy memories, recalling only the disappointments and anxiety. It seemed like I'd always been nervous and, glancing down at my fingernails, I realized that I'd been chewing them off since I was a little kid, around about the time of the hockey incident.

I had wanted to play hockey since I'd started school, and every year I had told my friends that I would be joining the league. Then the season would start without me, so I'd claim that I'd be joining later in the winter. Then it would be after Christmas, and finally, the next season. In grade four it almost happened.

I was in town with Dad one Saturday, and of course he had to make a stop at the liquor store, which was just two doors away from the sporting goods store. I mustered the courage to suggest we go in and look at the hockey equipment, and he surprised me by agreeing. Much more surprising, I walked out of there with a pair of shin pads and

24

a helmet. It had been too late in the year to join the league, but I was ready for next year, and there was no turning back. It felt like I'd started a whole new life, one where I actually mattered more than booze.

I guess I should've known there was something wrong when we pulled into our yard. "Don't let your mother see them," Dad had said, indicating the hockey gear with a nod of his head. "She'll be pissed."

Why would she be mad? Didn't she know how great it would be, watching her son streak down the ice, "Baldwin" emblazoned across the back of his jersey, scoring another game-winning goal? Why would she be angry about that?

I was watching television with Jenny later that evening, when Mom went into my bedroom for something or other. My hockey gear was lying on the bed where I'd carelessly left it, and she brought it out to the living room.

"What's this?" she demanded, holding the pads and helmet up so that there could be no mistaking what she was referring to.

"It's my hockey equipment," I replied, feeling like my heart had stopped.

"We can't afford it. It'll have to go back. For God's sake, Jacob, you know better than that. We can hardly afford to eat and keep a roof over our head as it is. Monday morning it'll have to go back."

Just like that. I didn't even bother to argue about it, I just went to my room for my Master

Magnet set, and then for a walk. As I walked, I
threw the pieces of the set into the woods along
the side of the road. It had been the best present
Mom ever got me for Christmas, but then it
became just a way to get even. Nothing had ever
been normal in our lives, everything was always
wrong. From that point, I was like the rest of the
kids who had a drunk for a parent, protecting
myself by making sure that nothing mattered.

Now the man who had created that life for me,
the man I'd learned to loathe, lay in a hospital
operating room, on the verge of death from his
own stupidity. I wondered if we all would've been
better off if he'd been alone when it happened, if
there'd been nobody there to save him. I realized
that was a bad thing to think, but couldn't seem to
dredge up any guilt about it.

I'd just finished my second cigarette and was
about to head back into the hospital when I saw
Aunt Corrine pulling in. I noticed that she didn't
drop off Mom at the Emergency Room doors, but
instead cruised around until she found a spot in
the shade to park.

Mom and Jenny walked over, and with one of
her patented sighs Mom asked, "How is he?"

"He's alive," I said. "At least he was when we
got here."

With another huge sigh, she said, "Let's go see,
Jenny," and they wandered in through the lobby.
Jenny had a book tucked under her arm, and
looked annoyed that she even had to be there. Like

me, she only tolerated Dad, and resented everything that he caused us to live with — the fear, the embarrassment, and the poverty.

"I'd better go in too," I decided out loud, and Rufus went to wait in the air-conditioned car with his mother. I sat in silence with the girls, and within ten long and uncomfortable minutes the cops arrived. After speaking to the nurse at the desk they came over to us.

"Real sorry to hear what happened, Mrs. Baldwin, but I'm sure everything will be fine. We need to ask a few questions. Are you Jacob?" one of them asked me.

"Yeah," I replied.

"Do you think you could tell us what happened, son?" he asked, sounding almost as if he was expecting me to lie.

"No," I replied, watching his face react to my refusal.

"No?" he asked.

"That's right, yeah," I said. "I never saw a thing. My cousin Rufus was there. He'll tell you what happened. I'm curious to find out myself, I guess I never thought to ask him. I need a smoke. Let's go outside, and you can ask him yourself."

Chapter 4

I leaned against the truck and lit another smoke, waiting for the cops to catch up to me. I guess that it was only normal for the police to be informed when someone is brought to the hospital with a screwdriver planted in his chest. I pointed out Rufus's location, and one cop went over to the car and brought him back.

We all got into the police cruiser — Rufus and I in the back, of course — and the cops wrote down separate statements from each of us, although both stories were the same. Well, with the exception that Rufus had actually seen what had happened. Dad had been trying to pop the cap off a beer with the screwdriver, and had taken a tumble, landing on the sharp end of it. I hadn't realized that Rufus had actually seen what had gone down, and was really impressed with how cool he was being. Even when one cop asked him if he was sure that it'd happened that way.

"Yes, I'm sure. I was looking right at him."

We signed our statements and they told us that we were free to go, "for now." You never knew when the cops might think that a crime had taken place, and they'd go to any lengths to prove their theory right. This time though, the only crime that had taken place was that of being drunk and stupid.

Three hours later, Dad was out of surgery. It looked like he would be okay. The screwdriver had entered the right side of his chest, well away from his heart, and the doctor said that he'd probably remain in the hospital for a week to ten days.

"He'll be off work for at least six weeks, though," he added, and I knew then and there that I wouldn't be returning to school, which started in a couple of weeks. I'd have to extend my summer job in the woods, and take over Dad's place cutting pulpwood to keep the money coming, because we could barely survive as it was. I wondered if he'd be able to drink while he was recuperating, and decided that he could probably manage it somehow.

Since there was no use in hanging around the hospital, we all headed home. Mom took the truck, and the rest of us got in with Corrine. As we drove, I couldn't stop myself from thinking about what life would be like without a drunk in the house, riding in an air-conditioned car and having no worries bigger than getting back to school in a couple of weeks.

It was too hot to cook, so we had a quick supper of tuna sandwiches. Then I gathered up all of the booze. There was half a quart of whisky and seven beers left, not counting the one Dad had been trying to open. I tucked that one away behind some truck parts as a macabre reminder, in case Dad didn't make it.

"I'm heading for the fire pit a little later. What are you going to do?" I asked Rufus.

"Maybe I'll go with you," he said with a sly smile. "You think Larry might be there?"

"Oh, he'll be there, all right. You sure you want to go?"

"Yeah, I'm sure." I guessed that it was up to him. Taking a good look, I could see that he wasn't as skinny as he used to be. Not by much, but certainly stronger looking, in a lean and wiry kind of way. And I really liked the new attitude that he was flaunting.

This time, when Rufus saw Larry, Rufus had a big shit-kicking smirk on his face, like he knew something that Larry didn't. It turned out that he did.

"Well, it's *Goofus*, back from the big city, eh? Did you miss our down-home hospitality, or are you just plain stupid?" Larry said when he saw him sitting there. This time no one laughed, as we were all pretty tired of Larry's act by now. We'd all suffered it for too many years, and were really sick of not being able to trust him, never knowing when he'd explode over basically nothing.

"Idiot," was all that Rufus replied. Then he stepped clear of the circle of benches where we were all sitting. I prepared myself for another heroic hammering.

Larry knew a challenge when he saw one, and drained his beer, smashing the bottle in the fire pit for effect. Then he walked to within striking distance of Rufus, and put his fists up. Rufus turned around like he had thought better of it, as if he was about to walk away.

Then Rufus whipped the foot that had been farthest away from Larry straight up and back, crashing his heel right into Larry's face, who went down like an elevator with its cables cut. Tough as he was, Larry bounced back up, spitting blood and charging right into Rufus, who effectively put an end to things by meeting him with a straight right hand to the guts. Larry sank to the ground again, where he proceeded to fight for air, trying hard not to puke. He lost the second battle, and you had to feel sorry for the guy, losing a fight that he'd started, and then spewing a gut full of beer. All at once everyone burst out laughing, and I knew that Larry's time as the alpha male of our pack was over. Now what would he do, having lost the one thing that had defined him throughout his whole life?

"Let's go, Jacob. Looks like the fun's gone out of this party," Rufus said. I collected our booze and said goodbye to everyone. Most of them were still gawking in amazement back and forth between Rufus and Larry.

"I'm coming with you," said Bobby, which was great because he'd just arrived ten minutes earlier, with a full quart of rum. Bobby and I had been best friends since we were little kids, and I'd always thought of him as the brother I never had.

The three of us went back to Bobby's place and sat in the barn, laughing and drinking until we all ended up loaded. It turned out that, after the beating he had taken from Larry, Rufus had gone back to Toronto and joined a kick-boxing gym, and had been at it for four years. Bobby lit up a joint, and I ended up lying flat on my face, outside on the grass, just breathing it out. When I finally came around it was one o'clock and time to go.

Rufus and I staggered home, stopping to take one more look at the accident scene in the shed. I said that I wished Dad had been alone when he'd fallen. Rufus told me that I didn't really mean it, that it was just the booze talking, but then he wasn't the one who'd had his dreams pawned to alcohol.

I gave Rufus my bed — he deserved it after taking down Larry — and lay down on a folded blanket on the floor. Even stripped down to undershorts, and with a fan blowing the night air across the room from an open window, I spent the next few hours alternately sweating and shivering. Rufus seemed to be having no trouble sleeping, which was evident by the steady stream of snores that I attempted to ignore.

Finally I got up and whacked him across the chest, which only seemed to make him snore even louder. I pulled on my jeans and stumbled outside. I sat on the step, lit a cigarette, and lay back, enjoying the coolness of the damp lumber on my skin. I was starting to come down, and could feel the first effects of a hangover approaching. Then I remembered the beer I'd tucked away in the shed.

With the outdoor light off to keep from attracting mosquitoes, I used my lighter to guide me in the darkness, quickly finding the beer and returning to the steps, almost giggling out loud at my resourcefulness. I twisted off the top, tilted the bottle back, and poured well over half of the luke-warm contents down my throat. Then I sprang to my feet and whipped the remaining beer and bottle into the woods where, much to my satisfaction, I heard it shatter.

My whole life had been, up to that point, dominated by drinking. The reason I had never enjoyed a normal childhood, the reason we lived in poverty, and the reason that each day leading toward the future was one to be dreaded, came down to one thing: booze. My father was lying in a hospital bed, lucky to be alive, and his family could hardly summon enough concern about him to even pretend that they cared.

I couldn't think of a time when my life hadn't been ruled by anger. Whether it was one of my friends, or one of my parents, or one of my friends' parents, or me, it was always there. We'd all accepted being unhappy as totally normal.

Sometimes when I looked at other kids, at least the ones who seemed less miserable, I'd be overcome with anger. Then I'd start thinking of revenge, and end up hitting someone. And as far as rules went, they were for breaking, because that would gain the type of attention I was used to. And the punishment for breaking those rules fuelled the already present anger, completing the cycle.

And then I thought of how I must have looked, in the middle of the night, as excited as a kid at Christmas because I remembered the beer I'd hidden. I was heading down the same road that Dad — in fact, that most of the men that I knew — walked, while those around them suffered quietly. I swore right there that I'd be the one to change all that.

Chapter 5

It was after four when I finally got back to sleep, and when the sun hit my face through the window at nine-forty, my first instinct was to roll over and stay sleeping. Instead, I got up, staggered through a shower, and had an instant coffee out on the step, making a mental list of what I planned for the day. Instead of having two cigarettes with the coffee, I had one, which I'd have to get used to doing if I was eventually going to quit.

There was no sign of the girls and, since Corrine's car was gone, I figured they'd already left for the hospital. The truck was still in the yard, but I couldn't find the keys, so it looked like I'd have to hitchhike if I wanted to go see Dad. Sunday morning certainly wasn't the best time to bum a ride into town, seeing as the cars were few and far between on our road even on a busy Saturday night.

I heard a vehicle slow down, and I saw Corrine's Lexus pulling into the yard. Jenny got out, followed by Corrine, but there was no sign of Mom.

"Is Mom at the hospital?" I asked Corrine.

"No, I dropped her off at the restaurant. She's working. She said there was no sense in going down there this morning, since your father will probably be sedated, and... well, you know... not feeling very well anyway."

"Hungover, she means," Jenny blurted.

"Mom went to work?" It was sad, but I understood that Sunday morning was the best shift at the diner where she waited tables, and that we really needed the money. Lots of people stopped at the diner on their way back from church. It seemed that getting all religious caused them to tip well, and sometimes Mom would average five dollars per table. I couldn't wait to explain to her that money was going to become much less of a worry soon. If I took Dad's place cutting pulpwood, I could keep the money coming in. And I wasn't even going to tell her about the score Bobby and I were sitting on. In a very short while, we were going to be up to our pockets in weed, which would quickly fill those same pockets with cash.

"So, *you* guys were at the hospital, right?" I inquired.

"No, we had breakfast and then took a drive, just relaxing and enjoying the air conditioning. I'd forgotten how beautiful it is around here, everything's so green and lush. Well, before we knew it we were almost out to the coast. Is Rufus still sleeping?"

"Yeah," I replied. "Why didn't Mom take the truck?"

"She said that she'd smelled something burning as she was driving back from the hospital yesterday, and that she'd forgot to mention it to you. I guess she didn't want to take any chances."

"Look, Jacob," Aunt Corrinne continued, placing her hand on my shoulder, "you people can't go on living like this. It's no good for anyone. Your mother was going to surprise you and Jenny with this, but I guess that doesn't matter now. She was planning on coming back to Toronto with us for a visit, and bringing you two with her. I'm sorry if you think it's none of my business, but it is my business to care for the people that I love, and I see where you're all headed. It's horrible, Jacob, and what's more horrible is that it doesn't have to be like this. I'd just like to see you enjoy your life, have some fun, do fun things. *Normal* things, that's all."

I didn't think she had any right to judge our lives like that, even though what she'd said was true. I wondered if she knew that her son was on the verge of abandoning her perfect world, but kept my thoughts to myself. All I knew was that I was going to try my best to make things better for us. "Would you drive Jenny and me to the hospital?

We'd like to see our father," I replied, choosing to ignore her attempt to meddle in our lives. To my surprise, Jenny nodded her head at me in agreement.

"Of course I will. Let me check on Rufus, and I'll be right back," Corrine said, and entered the house.

I went over to Jenny and gave her an awkward hug. Awkward for both of us, because I couldn't remember the last time I'd hugged her, if ever. "Everything's going to be all right, Jenny," I said.

I checked under the hood of the truck and found a tube of gasket sealer that we'd forgotten on top of the block. It had melted, and that was the smell that Mom had been worried about. I was relieved that it was nothing serious.

"He's still asleep, I left him a note," Corrine said, coming out of the house. "I can't believe him, sleeping this late. Rufus never sleeps in, and it's certainly not what you'd call cool in that bedroom. You guys ready?"

Corrine dropped us off at the hospital, saying that she'd pick us up in a few hours. I asked the lady at the information desk what room Dad was in, and we took the stairs up to the second floor. Visiting hours didn't start until two o'clock, but a nurse on the floor said that, since we were family, we could go right in.

As soon as I saw him, the reality of how close he'd come to dying hit me. He had an intravenous drip in one hand, and an oxygen line connected to his nose, and there was a half-filled bag of urine dangling under the bed frame, with a line running up under the blanket that covered him.

Jenny started crying, and I wasn't far behind, although I managed to keep it down to a hard frown and stinging eyes. This was our father, a man we lived with but hardly knew, and most of the time hated. He looked so helpless and weak, and I was glad that he wasn't awake, because I wouldn't have known what to do if he were.

After a few minutes of standing and staring, I put my hand on his arm and leaned down, whispering into his ear, almost embarrassed for Jenny to hear what I had to say.

"I'm sorry, Dad. You'll be all right. I'm going to stay in the woods until you're better. I've got it all figured out. Everything's fine, just relax. Here's Jenny." It didn't seem like much, and he didn't respond, so I could only hope that he knew how much I cared, because I actually did.

Jenny slipped her hand delicately into his, and said, "I love you, Daddy. Please don't die." She was blinking really hard, and looking the way that a little girl should when her father has just escaped death. To our surprise, he groaned and squeezed her hand. I pulled a chair up next to the bed, and told her to stay with him while I went to see if I could find a doctor. I also got her a washcloth from the bathroom, which I'd soaked in cold water so that she could keep his forehead cool, at least.

As I was walking down the hallway, I saw a

room marked *Chapel* and entered it, although I didn't know why. The wood-panelled room had fake stained-glass windows in the walls, and was cool and dark. There was no one else there, so I took a seat and sat staring at my hands in the dim light, my mind a complete blank. Religion was a mystery to me, even though I had attended church for a while as a kid. All I remembered was how boring it had been, and how fake the minister and the elders had seemed, with their permanent smiles and condescending ways. Dad had always said that they were worse than people who didn't go to church, because they *were* just faking it, out of fear of what might happen to them if they didn't.

I got to thinking about one time, when I was ten years old, and there had been a house fire. A woman had been in the hospital, and the night before she was to come home her husband had fallen asleep watching TV. He'd been heating grease to make French fries, and it had burst into flames. He and both of their kids, seven and three years old, had died.

The next Sunday the minister had spoken about the tragedy, and how it was all a part of God's plan. He said that, even though we couldn't understand His ways, we still had to believe.

At that point Dad stood up and said, "Bullshit. Tell that to the mother," then walked out. Mom picked up Jenny, grabbed me by the hand, and followed him. There'd been a lot of yelling on the way home, and I remember Dad saying something about there being no God, only fate.

I thought that he was probably right, because a God of love, who is supposed to protect us, couldn't be that cruel. Bad things happen to people, whether they believe or not. Maybe everything is fate, right from the beginning, and there is nothing we can do to change the path we are on. I hoped that he was wrong.

Chapter 6

I was giving myself a headache with thoughts that ran nowhere, so I wandered down to the nurse's station. I asked about the doctor I'd spoken with the day before, the one who'd operated on my father.

"Room 202, Frank Baldwin, right? And you're his son?"

"Yes," I replied, annoyed by her chipper attitude, although I realized that these people couldn't go around being depressed all the time by the horrible accidents and illnesses they are forced to deal with.

"That would be Dr. Walsh. He's on duty, so I'll page him for you. You can wait here, or he can meet you at the room, it's up to you."

"I'll wait at the room," I said. "Will he be long?"

"He should be along shortly, it's a quiet day.

You just relax, everything is going to be okay," she replied with a reassuring smile.

I returned to Dad's room where I found Jenny gently wiping his face with the cloth I'd given her. The smile on her face made me realize that, even though in her twelve years she'd known only hateful words and hurtful deeds from this man, her instinct was to love him.

"Did he wake up?" I whispered from the door, and Jenny swivelled her head toward me, her face all lit up.

"Yes! And he smiled, sort of. He couldn't lift his head, but he tried to talk. His mouth was so dry that he couldn't say anything, though. I went to ask the nurse, you know, if he could have some water and she said no. Stupid, eh?"

The whole speech was delivered in a hushed voice, but the look in her eyes told me that she wasn't as concerned about disturbing Dad as she was in letting me in on something.

"You know what I did?" she asked, and I had to smile, she was just so excited.

"No, what?"

"The cloth," she replied. "I soaked it in cold water, then I dribbled a little bit at a time onto his lips. Just until he swallows, you know, until I know he *can*. Wouldn't that freak you out, not being able to swallow? You know how dry he gets, Jacob. This is the same, except worse."

I couldn't argue her point, partly because I was so impressed that she understood, on her own, that

43

Dad was suffering a severe and silent hangover. I couldn't remember the last time that he'd gone a day without drinking. For some reason I'd thought that Jenny, lost in her fantasy world of books, hadn't been aware of that.

Dad had started to fail lately, I guess we could all see that clearly enough. He looked a lot older than thirty-seven, thin and haggard, and his attitude was that of someone who'd given up. The saddest part of watching him succumb to alcoholism, though, wasn't the physical breakdown. For me, the sickening part was watching him slowly lose his mind. Mostly it was childish behaviour after a few drinks, stuff that a little kid might find funny, like making faces and sticking out his tongue. Then there were the rants following completely idiotic lines of reasoning, like how we'd have more money if we didn't waste so much — even though there was no money there to waste, of course. We didn't even have enough for basics, with most of our money wasted all right, on booze.

He had also started to get really nervous, jumping at the slightest noise, and sometimes getting so jammed up that he couldn't be in the house alone. Like he was *scared* to be alone. All in all, it wasn't a fun situation for a family to watch develop. And it made him meaner to us than he'd ever been, but I kind of figured that the person he really hated was himself. Maybe now he'd get help.

"Jacob?" I heard a voice say from behind me,

and turned around to see a man in a white lab coat with a stethoscope hanging from his neck. "I'm Dr. Walsh," he continued, offering his hand, "I'm afraid I didn't even introduce myself yesterday."

"That's okay, thanks for coming, I know you're busy," I said. "This is my sister, Jenny."

"Hi," Jenny said, looking so guilty that I expected him to ask her what she was up to.

"The nurses say that he's doing just fine. They'll look after him, so don't you worry. You'll have your Dad back home and good as new in no time."

"Could I speak with you, in private?" I asked.

"Certainly," he replied. "Your mother isn't here?"

"No, she's busy, but she'll be along later," I said. I figured it sounded better than telling him that she really didn't care.

"I guess that makes you the man in charge," said Dr. Walsh with a sad smile. I followed him out into the corridor, where he took a deep breath. I thought that he was about to give me the bad news now that we were alone.

"Your father's not a well man," he began. "It's apparent that he's killing himself with alcohol, Jacob. He's aging way beyond his years. You are aware of this, I assume?"

"Yeah, of course, we all are," I replied.

"Well, it'll be a long and debilitating decline from here on in, for everyone involved, unless he takes the problem in hand. There's plenty of help

45

available, Jacob, but he's got to want to have it. The family will have to encourage him, and support him, and, God willing, he'll recover. I just wanted you to know that I'll do what I can, okay?"

"Yeah, sure. Thanks." I couldn't help but notice that he'd referred to God's will. If it was God's will that my father was an alcoholic, why would He change His mind now?

"He's got a punctured lung," Dr. Walsh went on, "and there was a pretty nasty chip to one of his ribs, but with rest and medication he should be fine. Because of his health issues, we'll be keeping him sedated, so don't worry if he seems unresponsive. I'll see to it that he stays here as long as possible. It'll give him a good start on getting sober. If you have any questions, feel free to ask, okay?"

I thanked him again and returned to the room, where I discovered one of the nurses checking Dad's pulse. I hadn't even seen her arrive. I had noticed that the nurses moved about the hospital as quiet as shadows, in soft-soled shoes, and could scare you half to death, showing up suddenly right beside you.

"We'd better go. Corrine is probably back by now. You can come down later with Mom, if you want," I said to Jenny.

"No!" was her only reply, and I didn't want to argue with her, seeing as how she'd assumed the role of Dad's private nurse. The real nurse said it was okay if she stayed, so I leaned over him and said, "Take it easy, Dad. I'll see you tomorrow."

I jumped back in surprise when he answered me, even though it was only a grunt. At least he was aware of my presence. I said goodbye to Jenny, told her one of us would pick her up later, and gave her a handful of change in case she wanted to get something from the vending machines.

Even though we were still in the grips of the August heat, when I stepped outside I could feel a cooler edge to the breeze that was springing up, a promise of relief from the smothering humidity of the last month. Fall would soon be here, bringing the promise of crisp mornings and cool evenings.

I would be working hard, but without school there'd be time for lazy, weed-inspired walks in the forest, hunting for partridge and white-tailed deer, not caring one way or the other if I even got a shot at anything. Bobby and I would sell our crop, and my family would be back on its feet to stay.

Of course, I'd forgotten about fate, and God's will.

Chapter 7

I saw Corrine's car parked in the far corner of the lot, and smoked half a cigarette as I took my time strolling over. I'd started smoking when I was thirteen, and in four years had moved up to nearly a pack a day. I realized that quitting would probably be impossible, but at least I could cut back until I got the booze under control.

"Where's Jenny?" Aunt Corrinne asked as I got close enough to talk to.

"She's staying. She'll go home with Mom later," I replied.

"If Angie even decides to come see him. I'll tell you the truth, Jacob, your mother has had enough. Seventeen years of it, and she's worn out. I wouldn't be surprised if she just packed it up and hit the road. A person can only take so much."

At least Mom's husband isn't facing prison time for being a thief, I thought. Besides, maybe this would give my father a reason to take a good look at his life. At least there was no harm in hoping.

I stayed quiet on the drive home, making a mental list of the things that I still had to take care of before the day was out. The most important of them was to get some water on the weed crop that Bobby and I had put so much time and work into. It hadn't rained for over a week, and even though marijuana doesn't need much water, it still needs *some*.

When we'd planted it, the plan was to buy ourselves our first pickup trucks with the money we'd make. I was sure that Bobby still intended to do that, but now I felt like I didn't have much choice but to pay off as many of my parents' bills as I could. It would take a lot of pressure off them, and hopefully it would give Dad the incentive to get straight.

Rufus was up when we got back to the house, looking like crap and claiming that he was coming down with a summer cold. Corrine just shook her head, letting him think that he was fooling her, even though you could smell the booze from the night before on his breath.

Corrine went to lie down, and Rufus asked me what I was planning to do for the afternoon. I really didn't want to tell him about the weed. It wasn't that I didn't trust him, but you never know for sure about people. Bobby was the only person I would trust with that kind of secret, and he felt the same about me. We didn't have to brag about what we did to make ourselves feel like big shots, although I knew that most people couldn't keep their mouths shut, and therefore usually ended up paying the price.

"I'm going over to Bobby's place. We have to, ah … we got something to do, you know, private," I mumbled.

"Oh, yeah, you guys are going to water that weed. Wouldn't it be easier with three of us? *I* can keep my mouth shut, you know," he replied with a knowing smirk. That's the trouble with booze, it causes you to mouth off and then forget about it. I wondered who else Bobby and I might've told about our crop; after all, we'd been drunk a lot of times since the transplants had gone into the ground four months earlier.

"Uh, sure. You may as well come along then," I said.

I called Bobby and explained that Rufus would be with me, and why.

"Well, yeah, since he already knows, sure," Bobby said. There really wasn't much he could say. We'd all been drunk together and, like me, he probably couldn't recall who'd first mentioned the crop anyway.

We met Bobby down by Miller's Brook, which we followed upstream a short way through the alders and hawthorns. There was a much easier and quicker way to get to our plants, but the last thing we needed at that point was to arouse anyone's curiosity. There were people who didn't grow their own weed because they didn't have to, people who would just rip off somebody else's crop every year. And the last thing you want is some nosy do-gooder following a trail right to your plants, and then tipping off the cops.

We had started out with forty plants, and were down to thirty-two, after losing the others to rabbits and deer, and even a few to slugs. That was okay, because we'd bought hybrid clones at the cost of five dollars each, and they were all guaranteed to be females, so we knew that every plant that survived would produce well. With thirty-two plants, at a conservative estimate of six ounces of high-grade bud per plant, we were looking at a harvest of around twelve pounds.

Bobby's older brother Weldon, who'd sold us the clones, was going to move the weed for us once we got it harvested and properly dried. We didn't have to get involved in the sale at all — he'd pick it up and transport it to whoever it was that he sold to, and we'd collect the money from him. At two grand a pound, we were looking at about twelve thousand dollars each.

Weldon lived in St. John, but made the three-hour drive home once every few weekends. He was totally cool, and no one messed with him, because not only *could* he kick any two guys' asses at a time, he *would*. In the world that he inhabited, you had to demand, and earn, respect. If you didn't, then no one would fear you, and you could expect to be taken down, or out, at any time. But you couldn't find a nicer guy than Weldon, if he liked you.

We had followed his instructions on how to grow the plants, and although it was a lot of work, it'd been well worth it. We'd shovelled dirt and carried manure for two weeks, creating ten separate growing plots, each one with four plants in it. Bobby and I showed Rufus how the plots were far enough from each other that you couldn't stand at one patch and pick out another although by this point in the season we'd created pretty clear paths between them. They were growing in an area that had been clearcut a few years before, so the abundance of young-growth hardwood trees camouflaged them well, while allowing lots of sunlight to get through.

Bobby and I had stashed four plastic buckets under an abandoned beaver dam nearby, and the three of us took turns carrying water from the brook. We gave each plot eight buckets, and it was nearly suppertime when we finally finished. I didn't mind the hot and tiring work, and neither did Bobby, seeing that we expected to be well compensated for our efforts. Rufus worked just as hard as we did, which made him a good man in our books, seeing as no one had mentioned whether or not he would be getting rewarded for his labour.

We wandered back to Bobby's house, where his dad gave us each an ice-cold beer. Though I had told myself I wasn't going to drink any more, I figured one couldn't hurt. We sat in the shade of the barn, sipping the beer and innocently planning our futures, blissfully unaware that one of us would soon be dead, and that one of us would soon become a killer.

Chapter 8

Rufus and I walked back to my place, and after I ate I called Jeremy Shaddick, a guy who worked in the woods with Dad and me. I was going to need a ride to work, and he was the only guy I knew who showed up every day, bright and early. He was actually a party animal, but he could really apply himself for the three months or so that it took to qualify for Employment Insurance every year.

"I'll be by about four-thirty, you be ready. See ya then," he said. The line went dead, and I had my drive to work lined up. Now to make sure I had a job too.

I called the foreman, telling him the whole story, which he already knew, except that he had heard that somebody had stabbed Dad. He understood that we needed the money, and said that there'd be no problem with me taking over for

Dad for a while. I was glad that we were working on a private woodlot, because I didn't have the certification to operate a chainsaw on Crown land. Actually, most of the large-scale cutting on government land was done by mechanical harvester anyway; chainsaw harvesting was almost a thing of the past.

I made a few sandwiches for my lunch the next day, and filled my water jug. Then I filed the chain, cleaned the air filter, and put the chainsaw under the step with my gas and oil. I was pretty well ready to roll in the morning.

Mom, Jenny, and Corrine came home, and I asked Mom how Dad was. From the brief glimpse I got of Jenny's face as she stomped off to her room, I knew that it hadn't gone well.

"I didn't go in, I just talked to the nurse," Mom explained. "He's asleep anyway, Jacob, and I'm tired, okay? I just worked all day, I certainly don't feel like sitting beside a bed feeling sorry for someone who's nearly killed himself with his own stupidity. And don't look at me like that, you don't know what it's like. I'd planned a trip for us, you know, but now that idea is shot. I should've known better." I kept my mouth shut and headed outside before I said something I'd regret. I was sitting on the step smoking when Rufus showed up.

"I'm going with you," he declared.

"I'm not going anywhere *for* you to go with me," I replied. "I'm just going to relax, get to bed early, and head for work in the morning. My drive will be here at four-thirty."

"I know, that's what I meant, I'm going with you."

"To the woods? Are you crazy? Do you know how hot it is, how hard the work is?"

"It doesn't matter. It's only for a few days, until we go back. You know you could use the help, and I can handle it. You don't even have to pay me, all right?" he replied.

"Sure, then," I said. I knew it would be a different story when the alarm rang at four o'clock the next morning, but I went along with him, even going so far as to make more sandwiches and to supply him with some old clothes that he could wear. Then I decided to take some target practice. Deer season would be coming up soon, and I wanted to make sure my rifle was hitting true.

Rufus came with me, and I was amazed at his marksmanship. The rifle was a First World War vintage .303 with a brass butt-plate, and kicked hard enough to numb your shoulder. He told me that every fall his father and some friends went on a hunting trip, and that he had no choice but to go along.

"Actually, they hardly ever leave the lodge, but we always fire off hundreds of rounds at tin cans. I guess it's their yearly attempt at being macho," he explained.

I slept in my own bed that night, with Rufus taking the couch and Corrine sharing the bed with

Mom. As I stumbled out to the bathroom at four a.m., I smelled pancakes. Seeing that he wasn't on the couch, I suspected Rufus.

Entering the kitchen, I saw that it was Mom doing the cooking, and Rufus the eating. She hadn't cooked me breakfast since I was little, like maybe in grade two, and certainly never at this time of the morning. The birds weren't even up yet.

"I couldn't sleep. Here you go," she said, passing me a plate stacked with steaming pancakes. I knew that she had got up on purpose, just to cook me breakfast, and was too embarrassed to admit it.

Jeremy arrived right on time, and we piled into the truck and were on our way. Rufus immediately fell asleep, and I wondered how long he'd last in the heat and the flies.

We arrived with enough time to get organized and warm up the chainsaw before there was enough daylight to actually start working. By late afternoon it would be way too hot to be in the woods, so when it got really bad after lunch, you could go home, having already worked a full day. At least that's what you did if you were smart, and didn't stay up late drinking.

Cutting pulpwood is one of the most dangerous jobs there is, and also one of the hardest. For starters, you've got a fifteen-pound chainsaw that you have to handle all day, which is capable of cutting you to the bone, and beyond, if you make a mistake. It spews exhaust fumes and sawdust into your breathing space, and by the end of the day it feels like it weighs twice as much as it did in the morning.

You're always tripping over something and getting poked by sharp branches, and you've always got sweat in your eyes. And of course, you've got to pile the wood, which is really heavy.

We worked at a steady pace until about eleven o'clock, then stopped to eat lunch. I hadn't heard one word of complaint from Rufus, and he'd stayed right behind me all morning. I was sorry that I'd ever thought of him as a sissy.

"Is this what you plan on doing the rest of your life?" he asked.

"Do I look that stupid?" I replied. "I mean, I guess I'm hoping to go to trade school, become a mechanic, maybe open my own shop someday. What about you?"

"College, I guess. I don't know what I'm going to take yet, just as long as I get out of there."

"Home, you mean?"

"Yeah, 'home.' More like boot camp. Dad thinks he can tell everyone what to do, how to live their lives, right down to the last detail. Maybe he can take a look at his own life now, realize he's not so smart."

I didn't know what to say, and I had enough on my mind without listening to someone else's problems. "Yeah, anyway, let's get back at it," I said. We worked away until two o'clock, then went out to the road to meet Jeremy.

Chapter 9

When you work that hard in those conditions, you usually end up doing what we did after work — have a shower and pass out. We slept until nearly five, when Mom woke us up for supper. I'd been working with Dad, on and off, for most of the summer, so I was in pretty good shape for the woods, but poor Rufus was another story.

He shuffled to the table like an old man, letting out a groan as he lowered himself into a chair. His muscles were so stiff that he had to turn his whole body, not just his head, to tell me that he was glad I found his discomfort worth laughing at. I said that I was sorry, but probably would've sounded more sincere if I hadn't laughed while saying it.

"Where's Jenny and Corrine?" I asked Mom through a mouthful of ham.

"Don't talk to me with food in your mouth."

"Where are they?" I demanded, after swallowing.

"Don't talk to me with that tone of voice," she said sharply. "I've had enough of that attitude from you people."

I realized she'd spent a lot of years under a lot of stress, and I was used to her mood swings. It was better to let her enjoy her newly discovered assertiveness.

"Where are Jenny and Corrine, Mother?" I asked, dabbing my mouth daintily with my T-shirt. Mom and Rufus both chuckled, and I had a sudden thought of how little laughter there'd ever been around our table, in our house, or in our lives.

"Corrine is visiting some old friends, and Jenny is hanging out at the hospital. You didn't notice that she was gone when you came home from the woods? She got Corrine to drop her off there before lunch, and said she'd come home with you this evening. You are going, right?"

"Of course I am. Aren't you? You *are* going to see him, right?" She was scaring me with her lack of concern, almost like she really didn't care.

"I'll drive you down. Someone has to pick Jenny up anyway," she answered, still not committing to actually going to visit with Dad. Maybe she was afraid that seeing him like that might force her to admit to feelings that she'd long ago attempted to bury. Still, if she was only going down to pick up Jenny, there was no reason for her to go at all.

I told Rufus to take my bed if he wanted to rest,

and he said that it sounded good to him, but that first he'd make our lunch for the next day. I tried to give him the opportunity to back down from his offer to help, but he'd hear none of it. I couldn't help but feel sorry for him, all stiff and sore and so covered in fly bites that he looked like he'd been shot-gunned.

Mom and I drove to the hospital in silence. As she eased the truck into a parking space, I decided to try out the speech that I'd prepared on our way there. I wanted things to change, for us to have a normal life, and her refusing to visit Dad certainly didn't fall into the "normal" category.

"Listen, Mom," I began, before losing the ability to put my thoughts into words. I took a few deep breaths, staring at the dashboard as if the words I needed would suddenly pop up in front of me on the grime-encrusted vinyl. I just wanted to tell her that everything was going to be okay, but couldn't seem to say it.

Turning and giving me a tight smile, Mom said, "Well, let's go." As we walked across the parking lot, I wished that I could just give her a hug, or take her hand, anything to show support, but that wasn't the way we were. In fact, the more I thought about it, the weirder it seemed.

"I love you, Ma," I said, immediately wishing that I hadn't. It sounded strange, wrong somehow, and I felt myself blush. Without even looking in my direction, she simply said, "I love you too, dear."

When we entered the room, Jenny was reading

a book, as usual, her free hand lying on Dad's arm. It was hard to imagine that this was the same little girl who only days before would leave a room when her father entered it.

When she saw Mom she burst into a brilliant smile and whispered, "He was awake earlier. He asked for you, Mom. They're going to start cutting back on his sedatives tomorrow, so he'll be awake a lot more. They want to get him moving around a bit right away, so his lungs don't get filled up."

As soon as Mom sat down and put her hand on Dad's head he opened his eyes. "Jacob," he slurred, and I felt the involuntary twitch that always came when he was drunk and said my name. Now would come the cursing, and the rambling lecture on all of my shortcomings. Then I remembered that he wasn't drunk, and went closer to him.

"Good man," he said, trying to focus on me, and I laughed at how silly he looked. His hair was sticking up in all directions, and he could barely keep his eyes open. I thought that maybe it was the first compliment he'd ever given me.

"I'm going to quit, Jacob, the booze," he said before closing his eyes again.

"I'm glad, Dad," I replied.

I looked at Mom, who took a deep breath. Dad smiled and whispered her name, and I saw tears immediately spring to her eyes.

"Do you want to take Jenny outside for some

fresh air, Jacob?" she asked.

Jenny and I went outside and sat on a bench in the shade.

"Do you believe him, Jacob? Mom probably doesn't believe him, but I do, don't you?"

"Yeah, I do, Jenny. It's time for all of us to make some changes. Let's just believe that, and see what happens. Deal?"

"Deal," she said, smiling so innocently that I leaned over and put my arm around her. Then I lit a smoke, only my seventh of the day.

"I'm cutting back," I said to Jenny. "And as soon as I get some other things straightened out, I'm going to quit."

"I'm glad, Jacob," she said. "I don't want you to end up like that."

She knew that I was well on my way to being an alcoholic, and I suddenly wanted to be a good example for her. It was another good reason to get my life together.

After a while we went back in, and Mom said that we might as well leave, as they'd given Dad another shot and he was out for the night. We were all quiet on the drive home, and as Mom shut the truck off she cleared her throat, like she had something to say.

"This is our chance, kids," she began. "If he can't straighten up this time, he's lost. We're lost. It won't be easy. But he was a good man once; let's just pray that he'll be again. I know that you've missed out on a lot, but that's all in the past, so let's just leave it there. Anyway, tomorrow's a new day. Okay?"

"We can do it, Mom," I said, and Jenny nodded in agreement. My resolve to quit the booze, and the drugs, and the smokes would have to remain firm. It wouldn't be easy, seeing as everyone that I grew up with and hung out with was a heavy user. But the thought of having something to share with my father was exciting, even if it was kicking an addiction together.

Chapter 10

As luck, or fate, would have it, as soon as we got into the house the phone rang. Brendon Martin, a friend of mine, was wondering if I'd like to meet him at his place. He had lots of beer and wanted someone to get drunk with.

"No, I have to work in the morning. Sorry, man, but I can't be hungover. Thanks anyway." It felt strange turning down a chance to drink, and I knew that it must've sounded strange to him, too.

"You're kidding, right?" he said with a laugh.

"No, I'm not," I replied, slamming down the receiver. I wasn't sure who I was more upset with, him for laughing at me, or myself for wishing that I could just go and get wasted. Staying straight was going to be hard, and I wondered how Dad was ever going to do it. Well, at least I'd passed my first test.

Rufus had made our lunch, and put the water

jugs in the freezer, so I only had to clean and sharpen the chainsaw to get us ready for the morning. I was so tired from the day's labour that by nine o'clock I could hardly keep my eyes focused. I said goodnight to everyone and went to my room, falling into a deep sleep as soon as my head touched the pillow. The next thing I knew, my alarm was sounding, and then we were back in the woods again, slaving, sweating, and swatting.

By Thursday Dad was awake most of the day, and they had him moving around a bit. When Mom and I got there that evening, he was sitting up, talking to Jenny, who was spending every day with him. Mom gave him a careful hug, and I heard her say, "I love you, too." It was almost a whisper, so quiet we weren't supposed to hear, but Jenny and I exchanged surprised smiles.

"It must be hot in the woods, Jacob. How's Rufus doing?" Dad asked me. He was still a little groggy from the sedatives.

"He's doing great, Dad. We both are, now that it's not so humid. And he's finally got the soreness worked out. The cutting sucks, as usual, but I'm burning eight tanks of gas a day, so it's adding up. You all right?"

Mostly I was asking if he was okay with the booze withdrawal, and his answer not only told me that he understood, but shocked me at the same time.

"I'm doing fine, son. They've got me on some kind of downer that's keeping the shakes under control. And they say I'm getting out of here in a week or so, but I'm not going home right away. I'm going straight to the detox centre. They've got a thirty-day program there, and the arrangements are already made. It's time, son."

I was surprised at how excited I was to hear him say that. I'd always wondered what it would be like to have a sober dad, someone you could actually hang out with and do guy things with. It was definitely going to be different.

"I know you're planning on staying in the woods, and I know that you feel like you have to, but I want you to promise me this, Jacob. Contact the school and arrange it so that you can do your lessons at home, so you don't fall behind. It'll be hard, but you can do it. You're smart. There's no future for you in the woods, or for anyone, for that matter. You're going to need an education to get by. Promise me?"

"Yeah, sure," I replied, hardly able to believe that this was my father talking. I had thought about going back to school once Dad recovered, but knew that I probably wouldn't have. I'd always said that if I ever failed a grade I wouldn't go back, and I'd barely managed to pass the last two years as things had become more and more chaotic at home. But I did pass, and did stay in school. Now, by applying a little extra effort, I could actually attend trade school.

"There's more. You tell him, Angie. I'm starting to feel those damn pills again," he said, sinking back into his pillows and closing his eyes.

"We're going to Toronto for a visit, the three of us. Corrine's leaving Saturday, as Ralph has a hearing on Monday. She's scared, and worried, of course, and could really use my support. We'll drive up with her and Rufus, and stay until Friday. We can come back on the train. You kids have never been anywhere, and Jenny will only miss a few days of school. It'll be good for all of us, and you'll have a chance to see how other people live. There're lots of things to do in the city, museums and all, and you can get around on the buses and trains. What do you think?"

As Mom finished speaking, Dad had his eyes open again, and Jenny had a wide-eyed look. All three of them looked as if I'd be disappointing them if I said no. I was actually pretty excited about the thought of getting away for a week, especially from the woods.

"It sounds like fun, but no way," I replied. "I've made myself a promise, for all of us. And what about you, Dad?"

"I really wish you'd go, Jacob, enjoy yourself for a change," he said. "It's not like you can come and visit me once I get to detox. I'll be fine."

"No, that's the end of it," I said firmly. I was making a responsible decision, and felt really proud of myself. I liked the feeling.

The foreman found me and Rufus as we broke for lunch on Friday and handed me my cheque for the week. It was more than Dad and I had ever made together. Then again, we'd never worked full days like Rufus and I had been doing either. All of the hard work was worth it when I saw the look on Mom's face when I handed her the cheque.

We went down to see Dad after supper, and I hung back when we were leaving so that I could talk to him in private. After all of the planning of what I wanted to say, I found myself at a loss for words. I wished that I could say that I loved him, but that didn't seem right. I wanted him to know how proud I was of him for the decision that he'd made to get himself straightened out, and how much I believed in him, but instead ended up saying, "We're going to be all right, Dad."

"We are," he replied.

As soon as I got home, Rufus said that Bobby wanted me to call. I hadn't seen Bobby since Sunday. He worked over in Elmdale with his dad cutting cedar logs, and they stayed in a camp there all week because it was too far to travel every day. He wasn't returning to school.

"Party time, bro," he said as soon as he heard my voice on the phone. "Dad picked me up a two-four of beer, and I got a few grams of hash from a guy on the job. Come on over, and we'll get wasted."

"No, I'm completely played out from the woods. I'm just going to hang out, relax, and go to bed early."

"Wait. You're not even coming over for a quick

puff? You gone religious, or what? It's black hash, Jake. You just can't get that stuff around here, and the beer's been on ice for an hour. Come on."

"No, I'm real tired, Bobby. And, besides, that crap doesn't interest me anymore. Dad's going into detox when he leaves the hospital, and I was thinking that we might have a normal life for once. I figure if I quit too, it'll be a big help to him, you know?"

"Get real, Jacob. You're father isn't going to stay straight any more than you are. Who are you trying to kid? Come on over, man, and bring Rufus with you. Maybe I'll give Larry a call, and we can watch him get his ass kicked again. I'll see you in a few minutes."

"No," I said again. The thought of getting a buzz on was starting to sound pretty good, and I was anxious to get off the phone before I changed my mind. Up until this thing with my Dad, I'd never taken a good look at my own addictions. I had figured that Bobby probably wouldn't understand, and the sudden click of him hanging up the phone proved it. It was okay, though. I knew that Bobby could never stay mad at me for long. We went back too far for that.

Chapter 11

Even though it involved three girls packing and getting ready to leave, they managed to be on the road by ten after six, which Rufus and I agreed must be some kind of record. As we were packing the luggage into the trunk of his mom's car, I took the opportunity to thank Rufus for all of his hard work.

"Not a problem," he said. "Is that offer still good?"

"Offer?" I asked.

"You know, if things get too rough, I can come live here?"

"Oh, yeah, for sure," I replied, though I couldn't imagine him leaving his life of plenty in the big city for the backwoods of New Brunswick. We shook hands, and he got into the car as the girls came out of the house. I gave Corrine and Jenny a hug, then Mom.

"Jacob, I want you to know how proud we are of you, all of us," she said. "I know you're a good boy, I mean *man*, and I'm, well, sorry —"

I cut her off there. Things were going to change, and no one had anything to apologize for.

"It's okay, Mom. Have a great trip. I'll see you in a week."

"The truck keys are on the table. You be careful in the woods. I love you, son," she said, blinking back tears.

"You too, Mom," I replied as I turned toward the house. I stood on the porch and waved goodbye through the tattered screen door as the car disappeared down the road. I decided that, since I needed to find something to keep me busy and my mind off getting wasted, I might as well start with repairing the door.

I found the keys, and a hundred dollars, lying on the kitchen table. With the forty I already had, I couldn't help but think how happy I would've been if I were still drinking. Mom was showing a lot of trust in me, and I resolved to prove her right.

I kept busy until the stores opened by cleaning out the shed. By the time I'd finished, I had two garbage bags full of empty whisky bottles. I did a rough calculation, and was amazed to discover that their cost, when full, would've been nearly a thousand dollars. Now they were worth a nickel each. When I realized that the woods behind our house was literally paved with them, it was easy to see why we were so poor. Just then I heard a horn blow, and I went outside to find Bobby and his father sitting in their truck.

"How's it going?" I asked.

"Couldn't be better," Bobby said, holding up a beer. "We're making a run into town. You coming?"

"Sure." I had to go to the hardware store anyway. Bobby offered me a beer as soon as I got in, which I refused, then lit a joint, which I didn't. By the time we got to the liquor store, the hash had stolen all my resolve.

"You want anything?" Bobby's father asked me as he was getting out.

"Yeah, maybe twelve beer," I said, then thought better of it. "No, make it twenty-four." I'd quickly rearranged my plans. It was the weekend, and I could always quit drinking on Monday.

I handed him the money, and he looked surprised. "No whisky? I thought you was a whisky man."

I was, so I gave him more money for a quart.

So Bobby and I ended up at my place, with forty-eight beers in the fridge, a quart of whisky on the table, and Neil Young wailing on the stereo. The plan to fix the screen door, like my determination to get clean, was long gone.

Saturday blurred into Sunday. I woke up Monday morning to find more beer in the fridge, and I realized I must have taken the truck to town the day before. I couldn't recall Bobby leaving. When I can't remember stuff, it makes me nervous, so I had a beer to relax, then five more. I passed out until after supper, then got straightened up enough to chance another run to the liquor store. I almost went to visit Dad, but figured he'd probably be sleeping.

I paid one of the bums who hang out at the booze store ten bucks to get me a dozen beers and another bottle of whisky, then went home and got my stuff ready for work the next day. Mom called, and I faked my way through a short conversation with her. Then I got drunk again.

Tuesday morning I took the truck to work. I took four beers with me, and by the time the chainsaw had burned three tanks I was out of liquid courage. Just then, the foreman came by to see how I was doing, and I told him my saw was acting up. He fronted me a hundred dollars to get it fixed, and an hour later I had more beer in the fridge.

Wednesday evening, I was sitting on the step trying not to go back to the fridge for another beer, knowing that it was a waste of time. I had spent the day drinking and dozing, and I was just wondering when the last time I'd eaten had been when I heard a vehicle drive by. A minute later it returned and pulled into the yard. It was Jeremy.

"How's it going, Jacob?" he asked, passing me a cold beer. I opened it and downed half before I even answered him.

"Better now," I replied, and he laughed at my wit.

"What're you up to?"

"Nothing," I replied. "You?"

"Just heading for the booze store," he said, and so we did. I got more beer, and more whiskey. The next day, for sure, I'd get my act together.

"You got your licence, right?" Jeremy asked when he came out of the store with the booze.

"Yeah," I replied.

"Then you better drive. I'm getting buzzed, and I don't need another DUI," he explained.

We drove around the back roads for a while, but when we met an RCMP car we decided that it wasn't a good time for a booze cruise, and went back to his place. He lived all alone in a big old farmhouse out on Henderson Lane, and did whatever he wanted, with no one to bother him. After we shared a joint of hash and another dozen beers, I felt like I was back to normal.

"You not working tomorrow?" I asked him as we sat outside.

"Got my EI hours as of Monday. I'm back on the gravy train, man," he said with a smile.

I felt pretty loose, and decided that Jeremy was cool, just another one of the boys. I told him that I wanted to let him in on a secret, but that it had to stay between the two of us.

"Hey, whatever you got to say, I never heard it," he said. I felt safe confiding in him. That's the wisdom of alcohol.

"Me and Bobby got a kick-ass weed crop just about ready for picking," I said, "over by the old Daniels homestead, in behind the logging road.

The plants are like Christmas trees, except these babies are decorated with bud instead of shiny balls. We got the clones from Bobby's brother Weldon, and he's taking the weed off of our hands, so all we got to do is pick, dry, and clean it, and we're in the money. You ready for another beer?"

"I was born ready," Jeremy replied. "Bring the hash and papers off the table, eh? I think it's time for another joint."

"For sure," I said, and made my way unsteadily into the house, where I proceeded to trip over a curled-up floor tile and crash headfirst into the cupboards, cutting my scalp on a door handle. Blood poured down my face, and I went to the washroom to check it out in the mirror. I don't know if it was all the alcohol in my system, but I couldn't believe how bad such a small cut was bleeding.

I returned to the porch with the beer and hash, a wad of toilet paper pressed to my scalp to staunch the blood. Jeremy had a great laugh, saying that I was as bad as he was, always getting banged up when I was drinking.

"That's just part of the game, man, ain't no big deal," he said. "Guys like us don't give a shit, right? Me, I could cut my hand off and not care, except that I couldn't roll then, you know? That'd be a bummer, for sure."

I found that really funny, and rocked in my chair as I laughed myself dizzy. When you're high, the stupidest things can get you going, and you laugh until it hurts, literally. I finally got a grip on myself and had a haul off the joint he'd rolled.

"So, where you guys gonna dry this stuff? You know, it gotta be done right, else it'll mould, eh?" he asked as I filled my lungs with the pungent smoke and held it as long as I could, then expelled it in a fit of coughing.

"In the hayloft, in the barn, at Bobby's dad's place. We don't even have to move it. Weldon's gonna pick it up right there."

"You guys have got it together, you know that? You're all right, Baldwin. Here's to ya," he said, tapping his beer bottle against mine. I suddenly realized that I must be. Why else would a guy ten years older than I was be sitting there getting buzzed with me?

Chapter 12

When I came to, the first thing that I had to do was figure out where I was. It's not a good feeling to wake up in a strange place and not remember where you are, but when I saw Jeremy's car through the porch window it all started coming back to me. My head felt weird, and when I reached up to touch it there was a hard lump of something stuck to the top of my skull.

In the bathroom I discovered that the object on my head was a blood-soaked ball of toilet paper, crusted solid where it had dried. *Right*, I thought, *the cupboard door.* I soaked it until it got soft and I could peel it off, but the cut started bleeding again, so I had to hold a washcloth on it to stop the flow.

Returning to the porch with a cold beer from the fridge, I came up blank on a lot of the evening before, especially the part where I'd passed out.

Then it hit me. I'd been drunk for days, I was supposed to be at work, and I hadn't even visited Dad. I quelled the attack of nerves these realizations brought on by downing the beer and starting another.

"Mornin'," I heard, and looked around to see Jeremy coming toward me with a beer in one hand and a joint in the other.

"Yeah, it sure is," I replied, taking the joint that he offered and filling my lungs. The head rush nearly toppled me off of the chair, and I leaned back and closed my eyes. I was aware of Jeremy moving about, and the car leaving the yard, but I couldn't respond. I came to when he kicked my feet and passed me another beer.

"She's a great day. Rise and shine, young fellow," he smirked, as if he knew something I didn't. "You slept another three hours. C'mon, I need the company. I got more beer."

So we sat and talked about nothing, or at least nothing important. I had two more beers and a shot of whisky, got sick, and asked Jeremy to drive me home. I knew that I had to get straightened up so I could visit Dad and get myself to work in the morning. My head probably needed stitches, but I could hide the wound with a hat, and it would heal by itself quickly enough.

On the drive home, Jeremy's car reeked of fresh marijuana, jolting me into recalling that I'd told him about our weed crop. I was glad that I was right about him not going to the cops about a little weed. But a little bit of worry started nibbling around the edges of my aching brain. I mentioned that I liked his air freshener.

"Yeah, great, ain't it?" he laughed. "Just a little deal I pulled while you were passed out. Keep it to yourself, though, okay? I know you're solid."

When I got to my place I immediately showered, then tried to eat a slice of toast, but my stomach revolted. I found five beers in the fridge, popped one to sip on to calm my stomach, and poured the other four down the sink. This would be my first sober day, the most important one.

I lay down on the couch, and woke up in the middle of the afternoon drenched in sweat. I finished the beer that I'd opened, showered again, and drove to the hospital. Dad was asleep when I got there, so I headed back home, thinking how stupid I had been to pour out those four beers. It had seemed like a good idea, but now I had nothing to help ease me off of the spree I'd been on.

I spent the evening cleaning up the house, trying to keep busy so that I wouldn't have to think of the mess I'd made of my week alone. It didn't work. I checked the oil in the truck and discovered it was so low that it was lucky I hadn't tried the engine.

I went to bed proud of the fact that I'd only had seven of the dozen beers I'd picked up on the way home. I awoke at five o'clock the next morning, had a shot of whisky, chased it with a beer, and went to work. I suffered through a full day, somehow resisting the urge to go home early. There'd be only one reason to go home, well, four, actually.

When I got home, I showered and made myself a ham sandwich. I cut it into four pieces, ate one, and put the other three in the fridge. I had *one* beer, brushed my teeth, and drove out to see Dad. I needed to talk to him, badly.

He was asleep when I got there, so I pulled up a chair and sat next to him. After a little while he woke up, and I could see by the way he was looking at me that he could tell what I'd been up to for the last week.

"You don't look so good," he said.

"I know, Dad. I really messed up," I began. "I've been drunk since the girls left. You know how it goes. But I have to stop. I don't want to end up like — I'm sorry, Dad — like you. I just want you to know that from now on I'm going to be with you on this, okay? We can do it, right?"

"Together, Jacob. We'll do it together," he said. "I'm being discharged tomorrow."

I sat with him until visiting hours were over, drawing strength from the fact that I had someone to lean on. We talked about our lives, and how things were going to change, especially for Mom and Jenny. It was the first time that we'd ever really talked, ever really shared anything but blame and guilt and anger.

I went home, ate the rest of my sandwich, and drank the three beers I had left. I slept soundly all night, and awoke to a brand new day. A brand new life, I hoped.

I felt horrible, but knew that it would pass, and that it would be the last time I'd suffer from an alcohol overdose. It occurred to me that Bobby hadn't called. It was strange, but I was all right with it, because I didn't need the temptation. I spent the morning cleaning windows and mopping floors, then headed down to the train station to pick up the girls.

"How was your trip?" I asked as they stepped from the train.

Mom just looked at me and shook her head in disgust. It's hard to hide the fact that you've been drunk for a week. Jenny went into a non-stop rave about all the places she'd been and all the things she'd done. I was really happy for her, but I couldn't get a word in edgewise to tell her so.

As we were walking toward the truck I decided to admit to what I'd done. Mom knew anyway, and I figured that I'd feel better once I'd come clean.

"Mom, I messed — " I began.

"Give me the damned keys," she said, cutting me off. It was a quiet drive home.

When we got to our place, Mom stopped the truck at the end of the driveway and just sat there staring at the house, her jaw set firmly.

"So, uh, have they got a nice house?" I ventured.

"Have you even visited your father?" Mom

said, ignoring my question.

"Yes," I said. Well, I had.

"Did you work?"

"Of course." Again, it was the truth, sort of.

"What happened to your head?"

"Oh, the woods," I said vaguely. She didn't want to hear what I had to say, so why shouldn't I lie to her?

"Let me out," Jenny demanded. I felt like asking Mom if she was happy now that she'd stolen Jenny's excitement.

It was too tense around the house, with Mom slamming any door or drawer she came near, so I went for a walk to the river. When I got home, Mom was gone and so was the truck. Then I sat on the step, smoking, thinking about how great things would be with Dad and me both clean and sober. Right then, with my stomach aching and my whole body feeling shrivelled from dehydration, booze was the last thing on my mind.

I looked up when I heard a vehicle, and saw our truck pulling in. Dad was on the passenger side, right next to me, so I stepped up to meet him as he opened the door. I couldn't believe he was home. He wasn't supposed to be. He was supposed to be going to detox.

He looked pretty thin, and really white, and his eyelids were drooping enough that I could tell he was on something. I'd seen the same look lots of times on other guys, always when they were coming off a spree. They would go to the doctor and get a prescription for Librium or Valium, and my buddies and I always thought we had it made when someone stole a few from his dad. We never thought that they'd miss them, never considered that those few stolen pills could mean the difference between someone having a withdrawal seizure or not.

"How are you feeling?" was all that I could think to say as he slowly straightened up out of the truck, looking somewhere above my eyes. He was on downers, for sure.

"Weak," he said, taking a shuddering breath. "But I'm on the mend, Jacob. For good."

"Dad?" said Jenny, walking out of the house and down the front steps. "You're not supposed to be here."

Mom just stood in the door frame as Dad made his way into the house and onto the couch, where he plopped down and immediately passed out. It was just like when he was drunk, except that he hadn't kicked over anything, or punched any walls, or called down anyone.

Mom and Jenny each went to their rooms, so I sat in the chair next to the couch and kept an eye on Dad. I couldn't help but wonder how he was going to be when he was done with the pills. I figured that sooner or later he would have to come off them, and wondered why he was on them to begin with.

They're called downers for a reason: they slow you down. The scary part is realizing how much the buzz resembles being drunk. Maybe the doctor was staving off one addiction by replacing it with another, one that *he* could control. Or maybe he was a pill pusher. There are always a few of those around, and they have a steady clientele. Everybody is looking for an escape, it seemed.

I drifted off, and woke up when I heard Dad mumbling. He was twitching and shivering, so I went to my room and got him a blanket. As I was tucking it around him, he started and swung his fist backward at me. It caught me on the jaw, and I bit my tongue hard enough to draw blood. He may as well have been drunk.

Chapter 13

I spent the next few hours cleaning up the yard, then I decided to mow the grass. I had to set the blade on the lawnmower as high as it would go because the grass hadn't been cut for months. Then I raked the whole thing, getting four wheel-barrow loads of clippings, before dropping the blades down and mowing it again.

I went inside to find Dad sitting at the table sipping a cup of tea, his eyes unfocused and his head bobbing up and down. As far as I could see, he had just traded one buzz for another. I sat down across from him, but he didn't seem to know I was there.

"What happened to the detox plan?" I asked.

"I'm all right," he replied, staring at his tea. It was useless trying to talk to him, so I decided to go check on our weed crop.

I was forty feet from the first patch when I knew that something was wrong. I couldn't see the massive buds that adorned the top of the plants, but hoped that maybe they'd just fallen over from the weight. But hoping didn't change what I saw — the plants had been pulled.

In a near panic, I sprinted to the next plot, and then the next, until I stood beside the last one, stripped clean like the rest. Every single plant was gone, torn up by the roots. We had been so close to success. Just another week and we would've had it made. But now this.

It didn't take me too long to get my head together, to rise above my first reactions of anger and self-pity and take a look for clues to what had happened. The first thing I figured out was that the thief had probably stumbled upon the plot. The plants had been hauled out by the roots. They were big plants, almost as high as I was tall, and it would take a lot of work to pull them loose from the soil.

Most people would've come back with a hand-saw, or an axe at least, and chopped off the plants above the soil line. So whoever had found them might have just freaked at their good luck and pulled them out in a frenzy of greed. Once they'd found one plot, they might have found the rest from the easily followed trails between them.

Then I thought again about the fact that Bobby hadn't called me in over a week, which wasn't like him. Was he feeling guilty?

Still, Bobby couldn't have stolen the plants. I knew that for sure. I didn't really suspect him; I was just grasping at straws. But did he tell some-one? Someone who waited until the plants were mature and then beat us to the harvest? Bobby drank a lot, like me, but I couldn't be sure that he'd kept his mouth shut. But that didn't make sense; if Bobby had told someone, that person would have come prepared to harvest.

Then I suddenly remembered the smell of weed in Jeremy's car when he had driven me home. I felt ashamed of blaming Bobby, and had to admit to myself that, just to look like a big shot, I'd probably cost Bobby and myself at least twenty thousand dollars.

My mind raced for a way to make things right. If Jeremy *had* done it, he'd probably still have the weed. It would have to be dried, since he couldn't just sell a bunch of green plants, and there was only one place where he could do that. I figured if I went to his house, and his car was home but he didn't come to the door, and if that door was uncharacteristically locked, then he was the thief.

I went back to my place and inflated the tire on my old bike, tying the pump to the crossbar in case I needed to re-inflate it to get back home. I pedalled down Middle Road, cut through an old logging trail to Henderson Lane, and hid the bike in the bushes. I wanted to approach Jeremy's house from the woods, hoping I could catch him outside.

My stomach was churning, partly from fear and partly because I still hadn't got back to eating properly yet, and my heart was hammering. Trying not to overthink the situation, I quickly crossed the narrow field behind Jeremy's house, walked up to his door, and loudly slammed my knuckles into it four times, and then again. No one answered, and the door *was* locked. With the car in the yard, I figured I'd proven my theory correct. I suppose that Jeremy could have been passed out drunk, of course. Still, he never locked the door. I had just turned away to leave when I saw it. Right there on the porch floor, standing out proudly against the brown linoleum, was a clump of marijuana leaves.

I knocked a few more times, just to really piss him off, then casually wandered back to where I'd stashed my bike. When I was halfway back to the woods, I quickly spun around to face the house, and saw an upstairs curtain falling back into place. He might've thought he was smart and that I was locked out, but in reality he was locked in.

I returned home and called Bobby, thankful that he wasn't too drunk, and told him I'd be over shortly. I was ashamed that I had got our crop stolen, but I'd come up with a plan to get it back, and I couldn't pull it off by myself. If it worked, Jeremy would learn a lesson about messing with the wrong people's dreams. He might suspect it was Bobby and me, but he wouldn't see our faces, so he couldn't be sure. He'd have to admit to the theft to even challenge us on it, and nobody was that stupid, not with Weldon Glenwood involved.

I loaded my backpack with a few things we'd need and told Mom I was going out for a while, but that I'd be back early, and sober. She didn't look like she believed me, or even cared one way or another. I headed for Bobby's place, hoping that I was right about Jeremy being the thief. Whether he was or not, I still had to explain the loss of the weed to Bobby, and I knew that he'd be crazy to go.

I arrived at Bobby's, so excited by my plan to get our weed back that I hurriedly told him about it being stolen in the first place. Of course, he went apeshit, smashing a beer bottle on the barn, and then doing almost the same thing to his fist. After he'd quit cursing and threatening death to everyone in the county, I got him calmed down enough to listen to my plan, and he agreed to it.

I put three beers in my pack for him, and we walked all the way to Jeremy's place, staying off of the roads so that no one could identify us if something went wrong. Bobby had guzzled the three beers by the time we got there, and I just hoped that he could stay cool and follow my lead.

We waited in the woods until it got dark enough that nobody could identify us, if anyone did happen to see two shadowy figures moving around the place. My nerves were stretched tight, and I couldn't think of anything but that we had to be in and out quickly. Hopefully — *with* the weed.

After one last rundown of how things were going to happen, we slipped through the shadows up to the back door. The car was parked in the driveway, the lights were on upstairs, and we hadn't seen anyone move since we'd arrived. I left Bobby by the back door, and made a circuit of the house, carefully peeking through the windows to see if anybody else might be there. But with no lights on downstairs, I was wasting my time. I could only assume that Jeremy was alone.

I put on my ski mask and hid around the corner of the back porch where it connected to the veranda, and Bobby went to the front of the house, where the car was parked. I could see him through the window, and wasn't surprised to see that he didn't have his mask on. There was an old flowerbed made from whitewashed fieldstones at the corner of the house, only a few feet from the car. Bobby gathered three of the softball-sized rocks and immediately blasted one through the car's windshield.

Unless Jeremy was passed out, which was always a possibility, the first smash that he heard would be a puzzle to him, and he'd start looking out windows. But he'd have to come downstairs, and, if we were lucky, outside to check out the car, because the veranda roof would block his view from upstairs. A half a minute later, Bobby crashed another stone through the other side of the windshield, and seconds later I heard footsteps running on the stairs.

I looked over my shoulder and waved at Bobby, signalling him to circle around the house. I was exasperated to see that those last three beers had been three too many, because instead of following my directions, Bobby just stood in front of the car, smiling. Suddenly the door burst open and Jeremy flew past me. He was moving much more quickly than I ever figured he could, but at least he was unarmed.

The plan had been for me to trip him, then pin him face down until Bobby had scooted around the house. We would secure him with the handcuffs I'd made from two plastic cable ties before taking him back inside. Instead, I sprang after Jeremy, who started to spin around to face me as he heard me move. With no other choice, I swung a punch at him, which he leaned back from, losing his balance and tumbling to the ground.

I jumped on him and managed to get my knee on the back of his neck. Once I had him pinned, he quit fighting and just lay there. I looked up to see Bobby walking toward us, his mask hanging out of the front pocket of his jeans. I pointed at it, then at my head, and Bobby finally caught on through the beer haze. I hoped Jeremy hadn't seen him, but I couldn't be sure.

We had the handcuffs on Jeremy in seconds, while he begged us not to kill him. I was glad to see him so scared, and figured that we had things well under control. That is, until we dragged him into the house.

Chapter 14

We laid Jeremy face down on the kitchen floor, and I tied an old scarf I'd brought with me around his eyes as a blindfold. Bobby drew back his foot and kicked him square in the face, and my stomach lurched when I heard Jeremy's teeth crunch under the steel-capped toe of Bobby's workboot. It reminded me of the sound that celery makes when you snap a stalk in two, except that this sounded like a whole bunch of celery.

I pushed Bobby backward, bouncing him off the cupboards, and he held up his hands to let me know that he was finished. Jeremy was trying to push broken teeth out of his mouth with his tongue and seemed to be having difficulty breathing. I realized that if I'd been boozing, like Bobby had been, I'd probably have pulled a mean move like that too. Still, the last thing I needed was this guy choking to death on his own teeth, and we still didn't even know if he had our weed or not.

I signalled for Bobby to watch him while I went upstairs to scope things out. In a spare bedroom at the top of the stairs I found our weed, half of it cleaned and the rest lying on the floor beside a resin-soaked table, ready for processing. The garbage bags that Jeremy had used to transport the weed were stuffed in the corner, so I put the bags of clean bud, along with the untouched plants, in those. I was back downstairs in minutes, packing at least ten pounds of marijuana. Jeremy had actually done us a favour, saved us a lot of work.

When I got back to where Bobby was guarding our prisoner, I saw that Jeremy looked like he had suffered no further damage while I was gone. As I stuffed as much of the weed as I could into my backpack, I was thinking that maybe this experience would turn out to be a lesson for him. But then it hit me that I'd failed to think through one aspect of my plan, and that was how we'd escape once I'd cut his hands free.

But he didn't know if we were armed or not, and he'd probably be glad just to be alive. So I bent down and whispered into his ear, making my voice real raspy so he wouldn't recognize it.

"I'm going to cut you loose, and I want you to stay still. You'll live if you listen, so it's your choice. Got that? And don't ever mess with those boys again."

I hoped that he'd think that maybe Weldon had sent a few of his henchmen to deliver the message.

I knew that Jeremy was basically harmless, just a guy looking for an easy score to get him by. But maybe I'd get Weldon to pay Jeremy a visit anyway, just to remind him of how lucky he'd been to get away as easy as he did. A lot of people would have stomped him senseless for messing with their crop.

The main thing was that Bobby and I had our weed back. At least I hoped that it was our weed.

I sawed through the plastic cuffs with a knife from the kitchen counter, then wiped the handle clean with a dish towel. We left Jeremy lying there with the scarf around his eyes as we hightailed it for the woods. The scarf would be no clue; it was just one that I'd dug out of the coat closet at home, long forgotten by whoever had originally owned it.

We made it back to Bobby's place without being seen, staying to the woods. We even managed to get the weed into the barn and hidden without his folks seeing us. Bobby had blood on the toe of his workboot. I didn't know which bothered me worse, the sound of those teeth snapping off at the roots, or realizing that my best friend was capable of something so cowardly. Then again, if I had been drinking, maybe I'd have lost control and done something just as bad.

Bobby kept pushing me to have a beer to celebrate our achievement, but I knew that he just wanted someone to get drunk with, and that anyone would have been fine with him right then. So

I begged off, leaving him acting like a snotty kid and well on his way to being officially drunk. He'd be passed out in an hour.

"I thought you were cool," was the last thing that he said to me as I left, and I pretended that I didn't hear him. In fact, I was just realizing how cool I really could be.

I was back at my place by ten o'clock, and everyone could see that I was completely straight, at least those who could tell the difference. Dad was slumped in his favourite chair in the living room, smiling at a TV screen that I guessed he couldn't even see, since he could barely focus on me as I walked by.

He slurred something toward my back, and I ignored him as I went into my bedroom. I'd have thought that at least one of the girls might've mentioned that I wasn't stoned or drunk, but Jenny had her head buried in a book again, and Mom was sipping tea at the kitchen table, looking like a broken-down old woman who was beyond caring. I'd be glad when Dad got off of the pills, because right then nothing seemed any different from the way it had ever been.

I lay there on my bed, staring at the same cracked and stained ceiling I'd been looking at my whole life. How many nights had I stared up at the crumbling drywall, unable to sleep because of some uproar or other that had Dad yelling and the girls crying? That was the sum total of my childhood memories — yelling, crying, and fear of what might come next.

When I was little, Dad had always given me sips of whatever he'd been getting drunk on, and by the time I'd had my first real alcohol buzz from booze stolen by a friend from *his* father, I knew that I'd found my escape. Now it was all that I could do to keep myself from getting up and returning to Bobby's place to get drunk, because what else was there to do, anyway?

I lay there arguing with myself until I drifted off. The next thing I was aware of was waking up to a loud crash. The clock on my night table read 4:36. I was still lying on top of the covers, fully dressed, and was out in the hallway in seconds, expecting to find Dad passed out on the floor somewhere. Then I remembered that he hadn't been drinking.

Well, it turns out that it *was* him, and that he'd fallen on the floor in front of the kitchen sink. I got him onto his feet, steered him to the couch, and laid him down on it. Two little yellow pills fell from his hand to the floor, and I picked them up as he gave a groan that faded to a snore.

The girls either hadn't heard the crash or didn't care, because there wasn't any sign of them coming to see what was up. The concern they had shown for Dad had quickly disappeared when they realized that he was still wasted full-time. The only difference was that he had switched from booze to pills. I couldn't blame them.

I downed Dad's Valium, then went outside to

have a smoke and await their mellowing charm. I'd taken them before, but these ones were really strong, and I barely had time to enjoy them before I started to feel the paralysis setting in. It was a wonder that Dad was able to function at all. I returned to my room and melted into the mattress.

Despite having slept for six hours before having to rescue my dad, I didn't wake up until nearly lunchtime, and it took two cups of coffee and four cigarettes to get me out of the fog. I thought about calling Bobby, but decided to stay clear of him, since I knew that he'd be spending the day boozing it up. I didn't need the aggravation of trying to deal with someone who was drunk, and besides, I might have been too tempted not to have just *one* beer, and I knew where that would lead. There was no such thing as *one* beer when more were available. So I spent the afternoon puttering around the yard, keeping busy and trying not to think about drinking. I'd just finished eating supper when the phone rang.

"How ya doin'?" Bobby said, providing me with a double surprise. Not only was he still home, instead of at the logging camp, but he sounded like he was completely straight too.

"Great," I replied. "How come you're still there?"

"Dad's passed out, so we're not heading back to Elmdale until the morning. You want to come over? I'll slip the scales out to the barn so we can get an idea how we made out."

"Sure, I'll be right over," I said. It was great that Bobby was sober, and I hoped that maybe I'd had some small good influence on him.

The first thing that we did when I got there was to find the driest stuff that we could and roll a joint with it, just to check out the quality. It wasn't really dry enough to smoke, so we just kept lighting the joint for each haul, and within minutes of finishing it we were both laughing like fools. We would have no problem getting two grand a pound for it.

Bobby got on the scales, first just him, then him and the weed. Even with a further loss of weight to drying, we'd still have about twelve pounds of high-grade marijuana, worth twenty-four thousand dollars in cash.

We raved about our ingenuity, our upcoming bankroll, and how we were going to spend the money. We made plans to double our take the next year, and decided that we would have to get started on new growing plots the very next weekend. We got all pasty-mouthed from the weed, so Bobby went into the house for water, returning with two cold beers instead. I drank mine just to prove that I could have a social drink. But it didn't work, because all I could think of was getting drunk one last time.

By the time we had finished our beer, the two of us had the munchies, so we headed to my place where I knew there was leftover potato salad in the fridge. We stuffed ourselves, then smoked another joint and sat in the shed playing cribbage on a makeshift table of plywood and a flat-topped five-gallon can. At one point I dropped a card, and when I bent to retrieve it I noticed the dark stain on the toe of Bobby's boot. The sight jolted me. It reminded me of why I wanted to get straight.

Suddenly it was approaching dark, and Bobby wanted to get home to bed. He told me he would have to get up really early to make it to work on time, because the foreman over in Elmdale didn't put up with slackers.

Now that September had arrived, it had started getting cool when the sun went down. A light breeze had started up from the north, reminding us of the frigid winter that was coming soon. I could see that Bobby was trying not to shiver, so I grabbed my jacket from the porch.

"Here, your teeth are about to start rattling," I said as I handed it to him. "Hard to imagine that only a week or so ago it was too hot to sleep. Just leave it in the barn when you're done with it, and I'll pick it up tomorrow night."

"Okay, take care. I'll see you soon," he replied.

I lit a smoke and leaned against the shed. I had just taken my second haul off it when I heard a gunshot.

Chapter 15

The sound of the gun had come from close by, from the direction Bobby was headed in. By the loudness of the echo that crashed by me I recognized it as something big, certainly not a .22 calibre. Something like a .303, or a .30-06, both capable of taking down a big buck deer, or even a moose, with one shot. It wasn't an uncommon sound out in the sticks, where people started putting a little insurance for the long winter ahead in the freezer any time after the end of August, even though deer season didn't start until mid-October.

I laughed to myself, thinking of how Bobby had probably almost soiled himself when the shot went off. At least he didn't have to worry about anyone mistaking him for a deer, as he was wearing a blue and yellow jacket, and it hadn't quite turned totally dark yet. Still, I thought, there was no harm in making sure he was okay.

"Bobby!" I yelled, walking over to the edge of the woods. He didn't answer, so I yelled again, but the only reply was the whisper of the breeze through the trees. Feeling like my heart was frozen in my chest, I took off running in the direction Bobby had been going.

I stopped at the edge of the field and called his name again, and this time I heard something. It sounded like the last of the water going down a sink. I started running again, and almost tripped over Bobby lying on his back in the long grass, looking like he'd got the scare of his life.

"Man, get up, you almost —" I started. But I realized that this wasn't some outrageous prank when I saw the spot of blood on his chest. I dropped to my knees and slid one hand under his back, right into a pool of warm wetness, blood pooling from where the bullet had exited. Bobby was blinking slowly, and he gave me a strange half-smile, as if he were puzzled by what was happening. With another sucking breath, he whispered, "Don't let … die, Jacob."

"I won't, Bobby," I told him, but I knew it was too late.

I placed my free hand over the entry wound and, turning my head toward the house, I yelled, "Help!" as loud as I could, although I knew that it was useless. If no one had responded to the rifle shot, it was unlikely that they'd hear my voice.

Bobby started to tremble violently then and, with his teeth gritted tightly and looking me straight in the eye, he hissed one last word. "Bastard," he said, and then his eyes were looking at nothing, and I knew that he was gone.

I scooped him up in my arms and staggered back to the house, trying my best to be gentle with him, so sorry that I had lied when I promised him I wouldn't let him die. I made it to the porch door, kicking it hard three times, trying to get somebody's attention. I didn't want to yell again, it didn't seem right now that Bobby was so at peace.

I sat on the step, cradling him in my arms like he was a big kid who'd simply fallen asleep. I looked down to see water running off my windbreaker, and realized it was tears. I apologized to Bobby, but for what, I couldn't be sure.

I heard the door open and Jenny say, "What are you guys doing? You'll wake Dad up." Then she saw the tears, and the blood, and I heard, "Oh, Jacob!" before she dashed back into the house.

I held Bobby until someone took him away from me. There were flashing lights, orders being given, and questions being asked, all of it too real to be a dream. At one time I saw Bobby's dad standing by a cop car, looking at me accusingly, as if he knew that I was somehow responsible for his loss.

At some point it ended, and I found myself alone, sitting in that filthy shed staring into the darkness. Earlier, Bobby had sat across from me, laughing and making plans for the future. I hoped that he was still laughing. He deserved that much.

Pictures started to flash through my mind, like photographs tossed on a table, one at a time. Bobby and me excited at the prospects of growing a marijuana crop, me telling Jeremy about it, me smelling the weed in his car the next morning, the kick in the face, Bobby innocently heading back home only hours before.

I knew that the shot could have been a mistake, fired by a poacher unsure of his target, who had run when he saw his blunder. If it had been Jeremy, would he have waited to see if I would come looking, or would he have panicked and run too? I'd told the cops that I couldn't think of any-one who had anything against Bobby, because it seemed at the time like it was the only way I could shield myself from accepting any blame for his death.

If it had been Jeremy, then I could only assume that I'd be his next target.

I'd had a friend drown when I was eight, and another one killed on a snowmobile a few years later, and a guy in my class at school had hung himself, so death wasn't anything new to me. What was eating at me was that a big part of this death was my fault, and Bobby had always been like a brother to me. There had been times when he'd felt like the only family I'd ever had.

I sat there until daylight came creeping over the treetops, and by then I'd come up with a plan. I set out through the damp grass taking the long way around — straight down to the river, up the shore, then straight up to Bobby's place — avoiding the killing field.

I came up behind the barn, taking a peek around the corner toward the house. There were a bunch of vehicles parked in the driveway, but there was no one around the yard. I went in through the manure hatch in the back wall, retrieved the weed from where it was stashed under a hollow stack of ancient hay bales, and made my escape.

Later I would go over to the house for real, when I knew that Weldon would be home from the city, and tell him the story that I had come up with. Bobby had got drunk and spilled the beans about our weed crop to Jeremy, who had then stolen it. We had gone to Jeremy's to retrieve it but it wasn't there, except for the stalks that we found chopped up at the bottom of a garbage can, and Bobby had punched out Jeremy, who threatened to kill us as we were leaving. And now Bobby *had* been killed.

I would have at least twenty grand in high-grade smoke, which I could sell to any of a number of dealers that I knew, and Weldon would have no reason to doubt my story. He would refuse to listen to any begging or deal-making from Jeremy, and extract a horrible revenge on his little brother's killer. Jeremy's body would be sunk in the river, or buried back in a black spruce swamp, and that would be that. I would have vengeance for Bobby's death, responsibility for justice being served, and all the money.

I stashed the weed in the rafters of the shed when I got home, and focused on trying to justify the guilt that I was feeling over what I'd done. The reality of Bobby's murder, and the part that I'd played in it, hadn't fully sunk in yet, but I knew that I'd have to deal with it sooner or later. I realized that I'd picked a bad time to get sober.

When I entered the house, Mom was standing by the sink, her head tilted down and her eyes closed, but that didn't stop the flow of tears that were plopping into the dishwater. Dad was visible through the archway into the living room, sitting on the couch with a perplexed look on his face, as if he was trying to remember something. He still reminded me of a drunk, but at least he wasn't aggressive.

"What in God's name happened, Jacob?" Mom asked, without changing position.

"Bobby got shot. He's dead," I replied.

"I mean what's happened to us, to all of us, to our lives?" she said. "It's like we're all dead, and just going through the motions of living. Take a look in that room, Jacob. Take a look at your future. I swear, Bobby's better off for it."

I couldn't find anything to say, so I went to my room and lay on the bed. I got to thinking about Bobby and me growing up together, following all the wrong influences, until we had become what we were, escapees from life. Then I cried, as quietly as I could, until my T-shirt and pillow were soaked. I'd started out crying about Bobby, but by the time I stopped I couldn't have numbered the reasons that had gone through my mind. I really needed a drink.

I still had on the bloodstained clothes from the night before but at least I'd washed my hands at some point. I needed food and sleep, but I showered instead. We ran out of hot water long before I felt clean. When I went back to my room, Jenny was waiting for me, and I held her awkwardly as she sobbed into my chest. "Please don't drink, Jacob. Then Dad won't drink, and we can stay together. Promise?" she whispered, and I swore that I would stop drinking.

I went back to my room and sat on the bed, and before I knew what had happened it was the next day, the day of Bobby's wake. I almost didn't go to his folk's house, but in the end I knew that I had to, not only out of respect, but to make sure that Jeremy would pay for his crime. There would be no trial, just punishment, swift and sure. I tried to pick out some decent clothes to wear to the Glenwoods' house. I didn't own a suit, and my good shoes were too tight, but I'd have to wear them anyway.

Bobby's mother looked ten years older than the last time I had seen her, and his father looked like another drink would tip him over. They both hugged me and cried on me, but I was all cried out. They introduced me to numerous relatives whose names I didn't catch, and offered me food that I didn't want. It turned out that they had waited for Weldon to make the three-hour drive home before they'd gone to the morgue, so that he could identify the body, hoping somehow that he would come out and tell them that it was a mistake. But it wasn't, and he didn't.

I was having a cigarette with Sharon Taylor, a girl that Bobby had gone out with now and then, who was going on as if she'd lost the love of her life, when Weldon drove into the yard. I took a deep breath and reminded myself that it would all soon be over.

Weldon stepped out of the car with a bottle of whisky in his hand.

"Baldwin, come here," he ordered, and the look on his face made my stomach turn upside-down.

Chapter 16

I walked over to Weldon on legs that felt like they had no bones, and he shook my hand, then passed me the unopened bottle. "Crack that, and have a drink for Bobby," he said, and I had no choice but to obey. I swallowed three times and immediately felt the burning liquid spreading through my body, warming me like a wood stove on a frigid winter day. It felt like home.

"We're celebrating the death of two people here tonight. Bobby's, and whoever killed him," Weldon said so calmly that a chill raced up my spine.

My plan evaporated from my mind as I made a terrible admission to myself. *I* had killed Bobby. If I hadn't presented Jeremy with the opportunity to rip us off, which had led us to his place to get our crop back, Bobby would still be alive.

"Weldon, I need to talk to you in private," I said, indicating the barn with a nod of my head.

"Give me a minute," he replied, and walked toward the house.

I went into the barn where Bobby and I had spent so much time over the years. We'd played there while our dads got drunk together, little boys turning a collection of old barnboards and hay bales into a ship, a castle, or a pirate's cave with our imaginations. Only a few short years later, we'd turned it into a place to get high and drunk, complete with a sound system and a wood-burning stove for year-round partying.

I didn't hear Weldon enter, and when I suddenly became aware of his presence I jumped and threw my hands up in defence. My nerves were stretched tight, and I needed another drink to calm me down.

"You're all right, Baldwin," he said. "You remind me of myself when I was your age. Ready for action at the drop of a hat. We want you to be one of the pallbearers, since you guys were tight, like brothers. It's good that you were with him at the end. Here, take this, it'll mellow you out."

He reached into his shirt pocket, extracted a small glass vial, and shook out a single tiny red pill. He dropped it into my outstretched palm and handed me the whiskey. I washed it down with a huge swallow.

"You boys sure spent a lot of time out here, eh? I remember standing outside listening to you guys, thinking how great it would be if you never had to grow up. You know, that you could just stay innocent forever."

I stared at the stained and worn floorboards, as if seeing them clearly for the first time, just like I was beginning to see the sadness of the friendship that Bobby and I had shared for the first time. We'd just been two scared and confused kids looking for a way out, and going about it in all the wrong ways.

"Jeremy killed Bobby."

"What?" The look of hatred on Weldon's face made me realize that I was about to cause another person's death.

"Jeremy Shaddick. I think he killed Bobby." Then I told him the story I'd concocted, watching him grow angrier as I went on, until suddenly he smiled, although there was no joy behind it.

"Then tonight Jeremy dies too," he said, balling up his fists. "But, and I promise you this on Bobby's grave, his dying will take a good while. Have another drink, and I'll tell the folks we're going for a drive. You up?"

"Yeah, you better believe I'm up," I replied, even though I wasn't. I was scared and appalled, and wished that I'd never suggested to Bobby that we grow a marijuana crop. Now that events had played out, it was as if he had agreed to his own death.

I waited by the car while Weldon went back into the house, wishing that I could somehow escape the deception that I'd created, although I wasn't even sure what parts of it might have been true at that point. The booze and the pill weren't helping, except to calm me down so much that my emotions were becoming hard to distinguish from each other. Fear, anger, guilt, and grief congealed into one jumbled mass in my mind.

Weldon came out of the house and we got into his car. He turned the stereo up full-blast, and I squeezed my fingers numb hanging on to the door handle and dashboard as he defied the laws of physics on the drive to Jeremy's place. He stopped the car and shut off the music just before the house came into view. Reaching under his seat, he pulled out a sinister looking handgun, cocked it, slid the safety on, and handed it to me.

"I'll take care of this guy, Jacob," he said in a thick voice, "but you'll have your fun too. When the time comes, you slam one shot — just one — through his knee. You got that? From the back, blow the cap right out. Okay?"

It wasn't okay, but all I could do was say, "Got it."

As we pulled into Jeremy's yard, we could both see that his car wasn't home, although I was the only one secretly thankful for that. I wanted Jeremy dead, that was for sure, but I also didn't want any part of the torture that Weldon was going to put him through. Weldon hammered the dash with his fist, cursing and ranting as spit flecked the windshield.

"Are we going to wait for him?" I heard a hollow voice say. As if through heavy fog, I realized that the voice was mine. Under the sway of whatever it was that I'd taken, everything was becoming warm and soggy.

"He's gone," Weldon said, suddenly calm, but with his face set like concrete. "Or maybe he's hiding in there. Give me the gun. I'm going in to take a look around. You stay here. If anyone comes along, blow the horn."

He got out, slammed the door, and walked toward the house. It seemed like a long time before the sound of the car door closing reached me, and I watched him walk for what seemed like miles before he finally disappeared behind the house.

I heard smashing noises, wood splintering and glass breaking, and it seemed to go on forever, so even with the effects of the drug I knew that it had to be a long time. Then I heard three gunshots, and knew that Jeremy *had* been home, that Weldon had found him hiding, beaten him nearly to death, and then finished him off with the gun. I might as well have done it myself.

Weldon came out of the house, got into the car calmly, despite the fact that he was out of breath and soaked in sweat, and said, "We'll find him, buddy. We'll find him, even if we've got to cross the whole country. Are you with me, Baldwin?"

"The shots," I managed to say, even though my tongue suddenly seemed way too big for my mouth.

"It was a warning," Weldon explained. "Three

shots through his pillow. If he comes back, he'll understand."

I was glad that I had been given a reprieve from accepting responsibility for another death, and hoped that Weldon would take care of it himself. I no longer wanted to be involved in it any further than simply hearing the news that Jeremy had "disappeared."

Weldon backed the car out onto the dirt road and was just pulling away when he saw something in the rear-view mirror that made him stop. It was Neville Chambers, on his bicycle, which he rode year-round, even in snowstorms. He lived in a huge old barn that looked abandoned. Most people called him Crazy Neville, but he knew everything that was going on, and he was always up to date.

"Well, well, Weldon!" he exclaimed, pulling his bike up to the driver side, chuckling at his own wit.

"How's it going, Neville?" asked Weldon.

"It is what it is," answered the old boy, and then closed his eyes and mumbled something before continuing. "My most sincere apologies to you, my friend. May you have mercy, dear Weldon."

"Where's Jeremy?" Weldon asked bluntly.

"Why he's in jail, of course."

"And *why* is he in jail?" Weldon asked, sounding frustrated and more than a little pissed off.

"Breathalyzer number four. The afternoon of the day your dear brother departed to a place unknown. The RCMP tried to pull him over but he made a run for it and slid off the road. He took off on foot, but they caught up with him. He can't get bail or a hearing until next week. And that, sir, is the gospel according to Neville."

"You sure? The afternoon? *Before* Bobby got shot?" Weldon almost sounded like he was begging. He didn't want to lose his ticket to setting the world right, the chance to avenge his brother's death, and I didn't want him to either.

"There can be no mistake, I am sure," he replied, and went into another fit of cackling. Seeing no sense in trying to make sense of the old guy, Weldon tore off in a cloud of dust, his eyes wet with tears.

Chapter 17

We drove in silence back to the Glenwood place, where Weldon simply shut off the car and got out, leaving me sitting alone as he went into the house. A bunch of Bobby's friends — *our* friends — were standing around in the back yard, smoking and talking in small groups. With great effort I got out of the car and stumbled over to them, shaking a lot of hands and nodding my head a lot, since at that point I wasn't able to speak.

I was pretty sure that I had to go to the bathroom, so I wandered into the house. I was standing in the kitchen for what seemed like forever but couldn't have been too long, since no one had spoken to me yet, when it all hit me. I was wasted again, Bobby was dead, and my old man was sitting at the table with a beer in his hand and a bottle of rum in front of him.

"A sad situation," he slurred, then took a long

pull of the beer. It certainly was. Apparently, the pain of Bobby's death had given him the incentive to get out of the house and find some consolation with his best friend, booze.

I went back to the car and grabbed the whisky, then went to the barn, where I sat and smoked and drank, and didn't do any thinking at all. When I came to it was pitch black, and only the familiar odour of the barn told me where I was. I made my way outside by feeling my way along the wall, not having a clue as to what time it was. There was a single light shining in the house. I was freezing, and didn't care if anyone was up or not, as long as the door wasn't locked.

It wasn't, and I walked in to find my dad passed out at the table, Bobby's dad sobbing quietly across from him. On seeing me, he suddenly became very alert, as if he hadn't been drinking all day and half the night. I'd seen my dad suddenly "wake up" like that. It's an ability that all veteran drinkers seem to develop. The clock on the stove read 2:47.

"If I hadn't been drunk, we'd have been on the way to Elmdale," he said. That was all that he could manage before he lowered his head and resumed sobbing.

"Sorry," I said. "I'm going to lie down on the couch." I didn't wait for a reply, knowing how glad Bobby's dad would be to have me there, just like in the old days. How many nights had I spent passed out on their couch, too wasted to make it home? Too many, I was sure.

Weldon shook me awake at nine o'clock and bluntly told me to get to his car, he was taking me home. He seemed really mad to find me there, and didn't say a word on the way back to my place. I figured that maybe he was upset because I'd seen him show what he would consider weakness.

I got out at my place, planning on going directly back to bed. Mom was sipping a cup of tea at the table, and I braced myself for a show-down. But she surprised me.

"Good morning," she said pleasantly. "Will you have a cup of tea?"

"Yes, sounds good, perfect," I replied, which was a complete lie, but a small sacrifice consider-ing the scene that I'd been prepared for. I could only imagine what I looked like to her, and won-dered what had become of Dad. I'd been trying to find the courage to ask her what had happened to his plan to go into detox, but knew better than to mention it while I was still messed up on booze myself.

I took a sip of the tea and, as I set the cup down, Mom stood up and leaned over the table, looking at my scalp.

"You're healing well. You're young, so you still bounce back quickly," she stated, making it sound like she envied me the ability. "Myself, I don't recover as quickly anymore, nor do I even care to. There's no sense in it, only more hurt. I've lived and learned, Jacob, and now I have to prove that I've learned."

As I sat staring dumbly at the floor tiles there was a sudden sharp knock at the door. I smashed my knee on the table as my whole body jolted in reflex. I got up and limped over to the door, hoping that it wasn't the police, but of course it was.

"Good morning. I'm Constable Lang, with the Millbrook RCMP detachment. This is Constable Carter," the first officer said, indicating his partner with a nod of his head. "We're looking for Jacob Baldwin."

"You're looking at him," I said.

"Jacob, we'd like to ask you some questions regarding the death of one Robert Herbert Glenwood. Would that be all right? I'm sorry, son, I understand that you were good friends."

The guy was so heartfelt in his last statement that I felt sorry for him. I couldn't imagine doing their job, especially visiting a home to deliver news that you knew would totally devastate a family.

"Come on in," I said. "This is my mother."

"Morning, Mrs. Baldwin," they said in unison. Lang added, "We're very sorry to bother you. We know that it's not a good time, but we won't take long. We don't consider your son a suspect, but we really would like to apprehend whoever's responsible for this tragedy."

"Certainly," replied Mom, looking almost flustered by the presence of two sharp-looking young cops. "Would you like a cup of tea? It's

119

already made."

They both accepted her offer. So the four of us sat drinking tea and talking about Bobby's death, which the cops seemed to believe had been an accidental shooting. They asked a bunch of questions and wrote down my replies, and by the time the tea was finished so was the interview. Officer Lang said again how sorry he was, and his partner concurred with a nodding head. I followed them outside as they were leaving.

"Do you guys know if Jeremy Shaddick was arrested the other day for a DUI and resisting arrest?" I asked them.

"Not that I'm aware of," Lang said. "Why?"

"Oh, he's a friend, and I just heard that he'd been busted, that's all," I replied.

"Could've been. We just came back on duty yesterday," he said, climbing into the cruiser.

I immediately went back to bed after they'd left, sleeping until nearly suppertime. After a shower, I rummaged around for something to eat, just something to save my stomach, but couldn't find much of anything. We actually had almost no food, and I wondered if Mom and Jenny had gone for some, seeing that the truck was gone.

I had a cup of coffee and a smoke instead, and Dad came mumbling from the bedroom while I was sitting in the kitchen, staring out the window at a vapour trail across the sky. He dropped a sheet of paper on the table, looked at me in bewilderment, and shuffled back down the hall. I didn't really want to look, but I did anyway.

There was nothing dramatic to the note, just the fact that the girls were gone, not to try to contact them, they'd call, and that the truck would be at the train station, the keys on the dash. I guess that I knew then what Mom had meant earlier. I hitch-hiked down to the station and drove the truck back home. They hadn't even said goodbye.

Dad stayed in bed for three days, and I looked after him the best I could. He was in bad shape, physically and mentally, and ranted in his sleep, although I couldn't understand much of what he was saying. When he was awake he would just lie there staring straight up at the ceiling, sweating and shaking, and once in a while he'd call out Mom's name. I guess he had grown used to her nursing him back onto his feet, and he just hadn't known that the last time had been the *last* time.

I had two nights of wakes for Bobby, and then the funeral to attend, and I stayed in a zone of feigned indifference the whole time. Bobby looked like a plastic replica of himself, with his hair combed wrong and his lips all stretched like his mouth was trying to open but something was holding it closed. No one had ever seen him in a suit before, and it was weird to hear the older ladies comment on what a fine-looking young man he *had been*.

At the funeral, the minister droned on about life eternal and how that was what mattered, not this fleeting experience of fragile existence, hovering at all times near death. I looked around at my fellow pallbearers, each, like myself, dressed in a mismatch of outgrown or borrowed cloths. Larry Simms was in a grey suit coat, too tight in the shoulders, and a pair of blue dress pants designed for someone a lot taller. Gene Lovell stood beside him, feet afloat in shoes three sizes too big. Even Bobby's dad looked like he'd suited up at the Salvation Army thrift store. Everyone looked numb, and Weldon wasn't even there for his own brother's funeral.

Were we such a bunch of flatliners that even the death of one of us couldn't evoke emotion? Had we insulated ourselves so well against hurt that we could now feel nothing? I was wishing that the minister would hurry up, when suddenly there was a commotion at the back of the church.

It was Weldon, standing just inside the door, his eyes two pools of hatred, with his nostrils red and raw from snorting cocaine. Suddenly he wasn't cool anymore, and I realized that he never had been. He walked to the front of the church, turned to face us, and hissed, "This is only the first death. The show has only just begun, folks."

It was the most pathetic thing I'd ever seen, but only for a few moments. Then he walked over and slammed his fist into the side of the casket twice, and stalked out.

Chapter 18

The church was as quiet as … well, a church. I could hear Bobby's mother crying, and I could see a lot of people shaking their heads in disbelief. Those same people would be more than happy to tell the story over and over for years, and I hoped they'd recall how great the tragedy had been that'd brought them to the church in the first place.

The minister carried on as if what had just happened was a normal part of the proceedings. Soon we pallbearers were lined up in two rows of three, just inside the doors, ready to carry Bobby's coffin to the grave that awaited him. It was a great day for a funeral, grey and breezy, and a slight mist had started to fall while we'd been inside the church.

We got the nod from the undertaker, and a whispered reminder not to touch the handles on the casket, which were fake. I wondered why Weldon, who was supposed to be a big time mover, couldn't have made sure that his little brother got buried in a coffin with real handles. Maybe he didn't care. Or maybe he was just a punk with a false reputation. After all, despite Weldon's scene at the church, Bobby was still the only one who was dead.

The coffin was heavier than I could have imagined, and I wondered if I was the only one who was sure that we'd drop it before our trip was through. Going down the steps was the hardest part, as we were prompted by the undertaker to keep it level. We loaded the coffin into the hearse, which then drove to the gravesite in back of the church while everyone walked along behind. The wind died down, the mist cleared, and the sun flashed through the clouds here and there. Bobby's dad threw himself on the coffin in anguish as we pulled it from the back of the car, but then again, he was drunk, maybe he just tripped.

We finally got the thing placed on the apparatus that would lower it into the grave, and stepped back to listen to more drivel about Bobby spending eternity in paradise. Then it was over, and all that remained was to fill the hole with dirt. I figured that it would be a long time, if ever, before Bobby was honoured with a gravestone.

The six of us remained behind after the mourners had left, taking turns filling in the grave. The mound of dirt, which had been covered with a green outdoor carpet during the burial service, was soon almost gone. Tommy Dalton retrieved a bottle of rum from the bushes where he'd stashed it the night before, and everyone had a big smash, except me. Tommy poured a shot onto the grave.

Something seemed to have come over me since the evening with Weldon, and I had no urge to drink or get high. Bobby's death just had to have some kind of meaning, had to change *something*. I wasn't sad, or angry, or anything really, just numb. I was afraid to admit that Bobby was gone, despite the horrible proof of the sound of the soil bouncing off the pine box the coffin had been lowered into. Soon enough, that was finished, and I walked all the way home in my too-tight shoes, not even bothering to say goodbye to anyone.

On the trip home, I got to thinking about what it would be like to die, especially to be shot. Bobby hadn't seemed scared. It was more like he couldn't understand what was happening to him. Then again, I didn't know what had been going through his mind, except that I'd promised him I wouldn't let him die. What else could I have said? I was sure that Bobby had planned on living a long life, with a wife and kids someday, although I couldn't recall us ever having talked about it.

And where had he gone? A city with streets paved in gold, somewhere in the sky? Where lions lie down with lambs instead of devouring them? Where no hurt is felt, and no tears fall? If so, how would he pass the time, since eternity is forever? I dropped the subject from my mind as my house came into view, knowing what awaited me there.

Dad was flat on his face on the floor by the couch, and by his smell I knew that he hadn't bothered to get up to go to the bathroom. I breathed through my mouth and heaved him back onto the couch. Then I changed, got my gear together for the woods the next day, and sat on the back step, smoking.

I checked on Dad from time to time, leaving a beer on the coffee table where he could reach it if he woke up. It would save him a trip to the kitchen, but more importantly it would save him the chance of falling down and getting hurt again. Anyone who drinks to excess on a steady basis knows the dangers of falling down. Concussions, broken bones, or even getting an eye knocked out are all common injuries among full-time drunks.

I slept well that night, which surprised me. I got up early and was soon on my way to work. Dad was still on the couch, and I wondered if he'd be all right for the day, but really didn't care enough to stay home with him. The day passed quickly as I laboured in solitude, lost in my thoughts. I dreaded returning home.

When I got there, Dad was awake, sort of, with a fresh box of beer on the floor beside the couch. I wondered where he'd got it, but couldn't make sense of anything that he mumbled, unless *suminyaroob* meant something. We needed food badly, and I'd spent the day at work eating cold Kraft Dinner and bananas that were nearly black. It had always been the same — little or no money for food, but always enough for booze. No money for vacations, or sports, or fun, because he chose to spend it on alcohol instead.

I felt the absence of the girls, and the loss of Bobby, for first time. The three people who meant the most to me were gone. I was overcome with anger at that, and suddenly had the urge to go into the living room, wrap my hands around Dad's throat, and put us all out of his misery.

Instead, I put my fist through the drywall by the living-room door, tearing my knuckle on the corner of a wall stud. It felt so good, the pain and the release, that I moved to the kitchen and opened up on the cupboard doors. They were made from thick plywood, and accepted punches without acknowledgement until I was spent. My hands were split and swollen, and I knew that I'd be sorry at work for the next week, but at least I'd got things to a level where I could deal with them.

I went outside to recover and have a smoke, and decided after a few drags to walk down to the river, where I could sit and soak my hands in the cold water. It would get me away from Dad, and maybe give me a chance to straighten out some things in my mind. I could've really used a drink.

I couldn't get seated properly to soak my hands in the cool river water, and ended up lying face down in the long grass beside the small brook that emptied into the bigger water. I lay there, dangling both hands in the fast-running flow, listening to how quiet it was, the only sound the gurgle of the brook over stones. Bobby and I had walked each other to that brook, halfway between our homes so many times over the years that I couldn't count them. I could almost see him there, on the other side, smiling and waving goodbye.

Suddenly a squirrel started chattering close by, signalling danger to anything in the area. The only problem with the alarm system is, they are so paranoid that they consider *everything* that moves dangerous.

The first squirrel had just calmed down when another one started up, off to my left, then shortly another, signifying that whatever was upsetting them was passing by in a semicircle behind me. Probably a deer or a bear, just going about its business.

Then it was time to go home and face reality. Would I use my loss, my anger and fear, to get me going and start a real life, or would I go back to getting wasted in an attempt to blot out those feelings? I had to get Dad straightened up, and get him some help, and I figured that I could stay straight at least until I'd accomplished that much.

Suddenly I became aware of a presence behind me. Before I could swivel my head around in surprise and fear, something hard and cold was jammed into the back of my head, pinning me to the ground.

"Don't move," a voice hissed, and I knew that it was a gun barrel threatening to tear the skin from my skull. Bobby was dead and gone, and I was about to join him. I squeezed my eyes shut and waited.

Chapter 19

As my life flashed before me, all I knew was that I didn't want to die. The pictures that formed in my mind were all of unresolved conflicts, leaving me knowing that it had all been for nothing. I'd simply given up, too weak to assert my own will. At the end, I suddenly saw why my life had been wasted. I was weak. If I were given another chance, I knew that everything would be different, but now it was too late, and I didn't even know for sure who was about to kill me. If Jeremy was in jail, and Bobby's death had been an accident, then it had to be Weldon.

The seconds ticked by, marked only by the rasping of my breath as I awaited the explosion of a bullet into my brain. Would there be pain, would I even hear the shot? Would there be any awareness beyond my last breath in or out? All of the mysteries that death held for the living were about to be revealed, and fear was my only companion.

"I didn't kill Bobby," I said.

"You're pathetic, aren't you?" the voice spoke, and I nodded my head in agreement, hoping that maybe I could live a few more useless seconds if I agreed with it.

"You're about to die, and there's nothing you can do but feel sorry for yourself, is there? I'll be doing you a favour, won't I?"

I nodded my head again, and he yanked me to my feet by my collar. He was still behind me, and I still couldn't be sure of the voice. Then it hit me. It was Jeremy, speaking through broken teeth. He'd known it was Bobby and me that night at his house, of course, and it looked like I'd fatally underestimated him.

Now he had made bail and come to settle the score. But who'd killed Bobby? Maybe it *had* been an accident. Or maybe Neville had mixed up the days. As Jeremy went on, I realized the second option was the likely one.

"He saw it coming, you know, your *friend*. He said your name just before I pulled the trigger. He was pathetic, just like you, calling for a coward to save him."

He pushed me forward, in the direction of the heavy spruce woods, where a single shot would be muffled by the thick vegetation and ignored by anyone who might hear it. How long would it be until my body was found? And if it never was found, would that be proof to people that *I'd* killed

Bobby? Would my disappearance prove that I'd actually pulled the trigger?

We walked for five minutes, and I recognized trees and rocks that I had seen so many times before but failed to really look at. There was a huge granite boulder, shaped like a lopsided heart, and a pine tree that had grown so twisted and stunted by lack of sunlight that I felt sorry for it. These were the woods I had used as an escape from my life, preferring their quiet solitude to the chaos of my home. Now they would provide a permanent escape.

"Stop," the voice commanded, and I did. "Now, take ten steps and turn to face me. You can run, if you've got the guts to try, but if you don't make it, I'll blow your leg off and leave you here to die. For a coward like you, it's not much of a choice, is it?"

As I counted off the steps, it became clear to me that I didn't have the strength to dodge into the heavy woods and try to save myself. I could barely lift my feet, and I trembled so badly that I was afraid of collapsing. I would die a coward.

At step number ten, I turned and faced Jeremy, but kept my eyes on the mossy ground at my feet, still hoping that if I didn't see him he might change his mind and leave. It was my only hope.

"Look at me." He spoke almost kindly, as if he was sorry for what he was about to do.

I looked up to see Jeremy smiling at me, but the smile was more of a grimace, his lips all scabbed and broken teeth showing behind them. If only Bobby could have kept himself in control, maybe we both could have lived.

Jeremy was holding a rifle with the barrel and stock sawed off so that it resembled an over-sized pistol. I knew that it would have lost most of its accuracy, but at that range it hardly mattered.

"You little shits thought I wouldn't know who you were?" he asked. "That other punk had my blood on his boot. And the scarf, you moron, it had the initials J.B. sewed inside it. This is all your own fault, big man, for running your mouth. Now, tell me where the weed is, and I'll make this quick."

"At Bobby's place, in the loft," I lied.

He raised the gun, pointing it right at my face. The muzzle hole looked as big as a soup can. I braced myself for the shot, but he wasn't done yet. I guess that when you suddenly hold that kind of power over another person, you want to savour it for a while.

"By the way, my car is in Neville's barn. I was staying with him. He lied to you and Weldon about me getting arrested, and you both fell for it. A guy like that will do anything for booze. Tonight he's going to get drunk and drown in the beaver pond. I just thought you should know that. I might go after Weldon too, before I take off, maybe see how tough he really is. Anyway, you got ten seconds. Enjoy," he said.

Ten steps away, with ten seconds to live. I

closed my eyes and counted down my life, hoping that I was in sequence with him. I wished that tears weren't running down my face, giving him the proof he needed of my weakness. Was that to be my last thought?

The shot, when it came, sounded a long way off, and I collapsed into the thick carpet of moss and spruce needles that littered the forest floor. I felt nothing, and realized that the snort I'd heard after the shot was Jeremy expressing his disgust with me, and not the sound of my final breath. He must have missed the shot on purpose, just to see my reaction, and was enjoying the moment.

Would he let me go now, having gained the proof he needed of his total control over me? I knew that he wouldn't, he *couldn't*. With me gone, and then Neville, no one would ever know the truth. Suddenly, I made a decision.

With a burst of anger giving me strength, I sprang to my feet. I would die on my feet like a man, charging into the darkness that awaited me. But there was no second shot.

Jeremy was erect, but on his knees, like a suddenly shorter version of himself. There was a look of astonishment in his eyes. It was as if his chest had exploded from within, and blood spurted onto the ground as he toppled forward into forever. On the way down his gun went off, but the bullet that had been meant to kill me found a home in his thigh instead.

I looked beyond the body, trying to locate my

saviour, but saw nothing except the dense foliage that had been intended as my tomb. Barely able to get my legs to work, I stumbled back to the house, stopping numerous times to catch my breath. I kept looking behind me, thinking that any moment I'd feel a bullet in my spine. When I finally made it, I tumbled onto my bed and passed out.

Chapter 20

I awoke at daylight, reliving the horror of the evening in my head. I thought that nothing could make me snap out of the endless circle of my confusion, but when I went to the kitchen, I saw Dad.

Dad was barely breathing, and his face was swollen with alcohol poisoning. I called an ambulance and they came for him. I declined to make the trip to the hospital once they got him loaded. I'd made that trip enough times, and there was somewhere else that I had to be.

I left the house and returned to the scene of my intended execution. The coyotes had found the body quickly and, by the look of things, another night of feasting would leave nothing but bones to litter the forest floor, and not many of those, either.

My nerves were so jangled that every movement of a bird or tree branch in the wind caused me to flinch. I started to walk home, eager to get away from there, but I still had no idea what I'd do about the whole situation. My life had been given back to me, and I vowed that it wouldn't be for nothing. I decided that I would use Bobby's death to remind me how quick a life can end. If I could stay straight and make something of myself, he wouldn't have died in vain. I owed his memory at least that much.

As I was reaching for the knob on our front door, I heard a voice say, "Hey." I spun around to face it. It was Rufus, stepping from the shed with his clothes rumpled and dirty, as if he'd spent the night there. There was a single clump of spruce needles caught in his hair.

"I decided to take you up on that offer, cousin," he said, attempting a smile.

"Lucky for me," I replied. He didn't let on that he knew what I meant, and I didn't push it.

He claimed that he had arrived on the train that morning. But the train came into town three days a week, with one arriving the day before, and none that day. Especially not that early in the day.

I suddenly realized what Dad had been trying to tell me, mumbling, "Someone in your room." Rufus must have been sleeping there when I'd left for the river the evening before. He would have been awakened by the sound of me hammering the cupboards, and had got up in time to see me leaving. He'd followed me, and of course he'd taken the rifle along, being a city boy and scared of the woods.

Jeremy's disappearance hardly caused a stir around our neck of the woods. The cops asked a few questions, but guys like him are hardly ever missed. They figure he might've been responsible for Bobby's death, but until they locate him, that's all they can do.

Rufus lives with us now, and we're both in school, getting ready to graduate come summer. Uncle Ralph, who got off with a fine and probation, sends him a big cheque every month to pay for his board, but we figure that it's also an enticement to lure him back home. He says he might go back, but I doubt it, as he's enjoying a freedom that he'd never have in Toronto.

Dad recovered, then spent six weeks in a detox centre. He's had a couple of "slips," as they call it, but I haven't. Mom and Jenny came home before Christmas, to a peaceful and tidy house, and now the anger of lives in turmoil has been replaced by laughter. Real laughter.

Some nights — most nights — I lie awake, thinking about how things worked out. If Rufus's father had never stolen from his clients, Rufus would never have come to our place, and I'd never have invited him to come live with us. Because of that invitation, it is Jeremy who's dead, not me. Sometimes I think that I should thank Ralph for being a thief.

Then, sometimes, I realize that if Rufus and his mother hadn't come to our place, Mom and Jenny wouldn't have gone back with them. I wouldn't have been left alone to get drunk, and wouldn't have ended up at Jeremy's place, spilling my guts about the weed crop. And Bobby wouldn't have kicked Jeremy in the face, and would still be alive. No matter how I look at it, Ralph, like all of us, had no idea how far-reaching the effects of his actions were going to be. How could he? How can any of us?

In the spring after Bobby's death, he received a new gravestone, donated anonymously. The cement base that it rests on is larger than usual, and was mysteriously put in place prior to the stone's delivery. On the stone itself is an etching of two figures, dark silhouettes waving goodbye, or maybe hello, across a winding brook. Along with Bobby's name, and dates of birth and death, there's also an epitaph. I like to think it's for both of us.

A life not wasted.